The Myst _, of_ 222 Baker Street

A New Sherlock Holmes Mystery

Note to Readers:

Your enjoyment of this new Sherlock Holmes mystery will be enhanced by re-reading the original story that inspired this one –

The Adventure of the Empty House.

It has been appended and may be found in the back portion of this book.

A request to all readers:

After reading this story, please help the author and future readers by taking a moment to write a short, constructive review on the site from which you purchased the book and on Goodreads. Thank you.   CSC

ALL New Sherlock Holmes Mysteries are FREE to borrow all the time on Kindle Unlimited/Prime.

The Mystery of 222 Baker Street

A New Sherlock Holmes Mystery

Craig Stephen Copland

Published by:

Conservative Growth Inc.
3104 30th Avenue, Suite 427
Vernon, British Columbia, Canada
V1T 9M9

Cover design by Rita Toews
ISBN-10:   1981342303
ISBN-13:978-1981342303

Dedication

To all those members of police forces throughout the world who have given their lives protecting the rest of us.

Hey Sherlockian:

You can have you name in print. Would you like to be a character in a future New Sherlock Holmes Mystery? I will use your name for: a hero (other than Holmes or Watson), a heroine, a victim (Careful on this one. You might not survive), a police inspector, a secondary bad guy, a secondary good guy, a servant or other minor character. If you do, then send me your name as you want it to appear and the type of character you would like to be to: CraigStephenCopland@gmail.com and I will let you know when you are going to appear. Warm regards, CSC

Dear Reader:

Do you want to receive notice of each New Sherlock Holmes Mystery when it is published? And hear about all free and discounted books?

Yes? Then please do any or all of the following:

Follow me on Bookbub here:
www.bookbub.com/profile/craig-stephen-copland?list=author_books

Follow "Craig Stephen Copland" and "New Sherlock Holmes Mysteries" on Facebook

Follow me on Amazon Author Central here:
amzn.to/2JOJVvt

Contents

Acknowledgments

All Sherlockians owe a great debt of gratitude to Arthur Conan Doyle. Of course, if you are a true Sherlockian, then the debt is owed to Dr. John H. Watson, who so diligently recorded his adventures with Sherlock Holmes. All of my stories are written as tributes to the parallel stories in the Canon.

This story is an attempt to write a locked-room mystery. In addition to Conan Doyle, I acknowledge the masterpieces of this genre by Edgar Allan Poe, Agatha Christie, Wilkie Collins, John Dickson Carr and other great writers in the past.

I wrote this story while living in the Okanagan Valley of British Columbia and must note my thanks to the Vernon Writers Group who reviewed the early draft and made wonderfully helpful suggestions. They and my invaluable beta readers have been incredibly helpful and encouraging.

My ten-year-old grandson, Asher Alexander Kuiken, helped me unpack and shelve my 6000 book library—a necessary task before I could return to writing. Thanks, buddy.

My best friend and partner, Mary Engelking, and my big brother, Dr. James Copland, read all of my drafts and suggest corrections, improvements and necessary cuts. Yet again, I am thankful.

Chapter One
The Old Order Changeth

Queen Victoria died the day before this horrific mystery began. Her passing at her residence on the Isle of Wight was not unexpected. We all knew that our dear Old Girl was not only getting on but had been in failing health for some time. And yet there was not a living soul in the entire British Empire who did not, like me, feel a profound sense not just of loss but of having become unmoored, adrift upon the sea of history.

Except for the elderly, all of us, male and female, young and old, light-skinned or dark, had never lived a day of our lives under any other monarch. She was always there. She was the constant North Star around which events great and small revolved.

The following morning, the newsboys were screaming out the news, and I bought a paper on my way to my medical practice. My immediate reaction was to ache for the company of my beloved wife, Mary, who had departed our home at the same time that morning as I had and was on her way to visit friends in Wimbledon. It was, I knew, a common human response when suddenly faced with sad news to feel a need to be with those who are close to you, and I sorely missed her company. Somehow, I carried on and fulfilled my duty to my patients through the remainder of the day, but as soon as my schedule would permit, I departed from my office and walked slowly over to Baker Street to be with my closest friend, Sherlock Holmes.

As I ambled my way through Paddington and Marylebone, I was inundated with the shouts of the newsboys announcing the latest. Condolence messages had been received from across the globe, and the papers were already trying to outdo each other with the news and retrospective summaries of all the events and changes that had taken place during the six decades and more of Her reign.

And, oh my, but how the world had changed. When I was a schoolboy in short pants, the great schooners and magnificent sailing ships gracefully bobbed over the waves and cut through the seven seas. Now they were long gone, replaced by steamships belching coal's black smoke and racing across the oceans at speeds that were previously unimaginable. If my father had wanted to send a letter to a relative in Australia, he could count on its arriving there two months later and wait another two months for a return. Now, a telegram could be fired off and a return received in less than an hour. The owner of a tea garden in Darjeeling could take his tea in the Windermere Hotel and read in the local paper the news of his home football team's win or loss on the previous day.

As I strolled along the wide boulevard of Marylebone Road, I pondered the sights and smells of London that had been part of my life since returning from Afghanistan. When, over twenty years ago, I first moved into to the rooms I shared with Holmes, the streets of London were packed with horse-drawn cabs, omnibuses, and carriages. The smell of horses and horse manure was omnipresent. Today, there were far fewer. They were being steadily replaced by the trains of the ever-expanding Underground, and, more recently, by motor cars, powered by internal combustion engines. Already there were several hundred of these vehicles in the great metropolis adding the distinct odor of their exhaust fumes to the air, and it was predicted that in a few more years, there would be thousands.

On reaching the corner of Marylebone and Baker Streets, I stopped and gazed north toward 221B. This familiar avenue was also changing. The Underground station had been installed and expanded several times and now served two lines. In the mornings and again in the afternoons, the doors of the station would open and both disgorge and swallow thousands of busy working men and women. Adjacent to the pavement, shops and tradesmen's stalls had come and gone. Across the street from 221B was another rooming house managed by Mrs. Hudson's friend, Mrs. Turner. The occupants of that establishment were constantly changing and, having moved away from the neighborhood, I could never keep track of them. The house immediately opposite my former abode, in which Holmes and I had overpowered the devilish Colonel Moran, was once again empty and advertised to let. Immediately below my old rooms, an enterprising couple had opened a sandwich shop and offered lunches delivered in under five minutes.

221B itself, thankfully, had not changed. Sherlock Holmes still lived there and carried on his now-famous investigations, dutifully attended to and fussed over by the long-suffering Mrs. Hudson. He still devoted himself to the relentless pursuit of justice and the undoing of an endless succession of criminals. For the greater part, he continued to act alone, keeping Scotland Yard at arm's length and complaining about their disappointing lack of imagination. Holmes and Inspector Lestrade, as always, tolerated each other but something there had changed as well. Now, when they found themselves in the same ring, they looked on each other in the way that aging pugilists do when facing their all-too-familiar opponent one more time. It was not what anyone would call a friendship, but Holmes and Lestrade had developed a grudging respect for each other, born of observing the dogged determination, the zeal, the unswerving integrity, and selfless passion for justice by which both of them were marked.

They also shared another trait of character: the refusal ever to give up. Criminals might have appeared to have escaped their clutches at the time of the crime, but time and again both Holmes and the Yard continued their relentless pursuit. Often they succeeded, months or even years later, in dragging villains to the bar. I have not put many of these accomplishments to account as they were not particularly dramatic and appealing to readers, but they were a passionate, if quiet, recurrence in the lives of both Holmes and Lestrade.

Inspector Lestrade, when he wanted to appear officious and assertive, would summon Holmes to the offices of Scotland Yard and assign him a case that he admitted was baffling to his dedicated assistant inspectors. Yet he would also, with increasing frequency, drop in to 221B to discuss some arcane matter or just to visit and pass the time with a man who, though unlike him in so many ways, was, in his heart, a kindred spirit.

It was just such a visit on 5 January 1901 that gave rise to a most puzzling and tragic case.

I had completed my walk to 221B Baker Street, and as I still had a key, I opened the door and entered. Before I closed the door, I heard a shout from the street.

"Doctor Watson! Hold the door for me, please."

I turned around and saw Inspector Lestrade walking toward me from the other side of the street. I gave him a wave and entered, leaving the door ajar. I ascended the stairs, and Lestrade followed me a few steps behind. On reaching the landing at the top, I turned to greet him, but my words were caught in my mouth. The man looked awful. His entire countenance was utterly distraught. I had known Lestrade now for over twenty years, and he had always been the picture of cool, detached competence. Never had I seen him like this.

"Good heavens, man," I said. "What is wrong? You look as if you just lost your best friend."

He gave me a look, walked past and proceeded into the front room and dropped his body into a chair without removing his coat.

"No, Doctor Watson. Not my best friend. One of my best men."

Holmes was sitting opposite him and immediately dropped the file he had been reading.

"One of your best men?" asked Holmes. "Inspector, please explain."

"My man … Inspector Forbes … has been murdered."

"Merciful heavens," I exclaimed. "I just saw him yesterday. That's dreadful."

Lestrade hung his head and slowly shook it. "Yes … it is. And he had a family, a wife and three children. I shall have to go soon and tell them."

Then he looked at my friend.

"I need your help, Holmes."

"Of course," came the reply.

"Thank you. If you could come straight away with me, I will take you to where it happened. Please, Dr. Watson, if you are free, come with us. Your medical opinion would be very useful."

"Most certainly," I said. "Let me hail a cab." I turned to leave and started back down the stairs.

"That will not be necessary," said Lestrade. "Forbes is lying dead right across the street."

Baker Street is a somewhat usual street in the residential area of London and comprised mainly of two- or three-story row houses. Some of the buildings are inhabited by the owners and their families, and others are let out to tenants who are of much the same class as Holmes and I were when we first agreed to share rooms. The house across the street at 222 Baker Street bore the pretentious name of Camden House but suffered from a lack of care and attention by its owner. For that reason, it was often, as it was now, devoid of tenants. Although I had observed the exterior of the house countless times, the only time I had ever been inside was on that fateful night immediately following Holmes's return from the dead, when we watched and waited for Colonel Sebastian Moran.

As Holmes, Lestrade, and I crossed the road, I noticed that two police carriages had pulled up and stopped, and a half-dozen constables had gathered on the pavement in front of the door. They nodded respectfully to Inspector Lestrade and then, recognizing Holmes and me, gave another nod to each of us, but no words were spoken.

"He's back here," said Lestrade as he led us from the vestibule and into the central hallway.

The house was entirely empty. There were a few decrepit pieces of furniture that needed to be put out for the dustman and some cheap paintings on the wall that no thief could be bothered to steal. The air was heavy with the smell of mildew and mold, and the paint on some of the walls was peeling.

Lestrade kept walking all the way to the back of the ground floor. The lamps had been lit and turned up, and we passed police officers standing at the doorway of every room. At the back of the house, we entered the kitchen and crossed over through a short rough door that led into a small windowless back room. I assumed it had served as the abode of a cook or maid but was now empty. There was not a stick of furniture to be seen. On the floor, lying prone in front of the hearth, was the body of a man. He was wearing a heavy winter trench coat, woolen trousers, and the type of boots that were commonly issued to police officers.

Waiting for us in the room was Inspector Peter Jones, also of Scotland Yard, who had worked closely with Holmes in the case of the Red-Headed League. The four of us instinctively stood for several moments in respectful silence. Then Holmes, in a manner that was most uncharacteristic of him, put his hands on the shoulders of Lestrade and Jones and spoke in a quiet and gentle way.

"Inspectors," he said. "Would you be able to tell me what you know so far?"

Lestrade nodded. His body heaved up and down again as he took in a deep breath.

"There's not much I can say. The estate agent came by just over an hour ago to check on the premises and found Forbes in this room. He immediately ran out and called for the local police. They came, did a quick look, saw who it was, and then sent for me."

"The house was locked, I assume," said Holmes "prior to the arrival of the estate agent?"

"Not only the house," replied Lestrade, "both front door and back, but this room too. The agent has a set of keys, of course, and he told us that the owner has the only other set. No one else."

I looked around at the barren little room. It was no more than twelve-foot square, with only one door, no closets or windows, and a small hearth on the back wall. Two cheap imitation Dutch paintings hung askew on the walls. The floor was dusty except in the central portion where numerous people had walked in the past hour.

In the only time I had entered this house in the past, I had not been aware of this room. Holmes and I had approached the back of Camden House by way of the alley that runs north off Blanding Street and moved immediately up the stairs to the second floor and the window that provided such a clear view of our rooms across the street. I assumed that the room in which we now stood had been closed off to ventilation for much of the past few months whilst the house stood vacant. It certainly had an odd odor to it that would have been disbursed by the application of fresh air.

If Holmes had remembered that night with Colonel Moran — and I am sure he did — he gave no sign of its having any relevance to our present situation. He already had his glass in hand and was plodding around the room, examining the walls and tapping against them. Then he used his stick to tap against all parts of the small ceiling and then the floor.

"There appears to be no other access to this room than through the kitchen and the door of the room," he said. Then he turned to me.

"Watson," he said. "Please examine the body and give the inspector and me your learned opinion as to the time and cause of death."

I got down on my knees and began my examination of the corpse. Rigor mortis had started to set in and was quite apparent in the eyelids, jaw, and neck, and just starting to appear in the limbs and torso. His face was still rosy, and his cheeks somewhat flushed.

"He has not been dead long," I observed. "No more than eight hours and possibly as few as five. It's going on six o'clock now, so that would place his time of death sometime between nine o'clock this morning and one this afternoon."

'You are quite sure of that, Doctor?" asked Lestrade. "The first constables to arrive here asked everyone they could find on Baker Street or in the alley behind if they had seen anything earlier today. No one had seen a thing."

"I have no explanation for how he ended up here," I said. "But there is no doubt that he has not been dead for more than eight hours. The rate of the onset of rigor mortis is well-known. He definitely died sometime between morning and early afternoon."

Neither Holmes nor Lestrade made any reply, so I continued with my post-mortem. There was no evidence of damage to any of the bones in the feet, knees, or legs. The same was true of the pelvic region, the spine and the shoulders. The back of his neck and his hands had not been harmed. With the assistance of a couple of the police officers, I gently rolled the body over. There were no wounds on the body and no evidence of bleeding that was of sufficient volume to have soaked through the clothing, which indicated that he had not died from a gunshot, or stabbing, or a garrote. His forehead and cranium were generally smooth, with every hair still held in place by a light treatment of Macassar. There was a small bump on the back of the skull, but no blow hard enough to kill him had struck his head.

I loosened some of his clothing and gave a cursory glance to his powerful torso. Again, there was nothing, and the skin was still faintly pinkish with occasional patches of pale blue. There was not a single bruise on his abdomen.

"He does not appear," I said, "to have been in any sort of a fight—no signs of a struggle at all. And no marks of any ligature or bruises on his neck. He was not strangled."

"Very well, then," said Holmes. "That eliminates a physical attack. The remaining possibilities are heart failure or poison." He turned then to Lestrade. "I presume that Forbes was not suffering from any fatal disease or a weak heart?"

"None," said Lestrade. "He was as healthy as a horse."

"Could he have been suffocated?" Holmes asked me.

I shook my head. "No. No man lies still and allows himself to be suffocated. He struggles violently. But there is not a bruise anywhere."

"Your conclusion, doctor?" asked Inspector Jones. "Poison perhaps?"

"Quite possibly," I said. "But as to what type of poison, I cannot tell. There is no sign of vomit or excess saliva. He has not soiled himself. So that rules out curare or some venom from the tropics. Arsenic takes far too long. Cyanide is a possibility."

Holmes dropped to his knees beside me and moved his body so that he could lower his nose to the mouth of the deceased and he sniffed several times.

"Cyanide," he said, "has a telltale scent of almonds. There is none."

I stood up and turned to Inspector Lestrade. His face had a vacant, dazed look and it was clear that his thoughts were elsewhere.

"Inspector?" I said

"Yes … oh … yes. What?"

"You will send the body to the police morgue, will you not?" I asked.

"Oh, yes. Of course. I will have a couple of the constables look after that."

"You might," I said, "ask them to tell the chaps at the morgue to look for any signs of a skin puncture. I did not see any, but I could easily have missed one. He may have been injected with a syringe."

"Yes. Right. Sorry not to have been paying attention. I'm afraid my mind has been on what I am going to say to his wife and children."

I wished that I could have offered some magic words of comfort to pass along. But there are none. As a doctor, I had learned years ago that the best course was to speak in as kind and gentle manner as possible and give the bereaved a factual account of what had taken place. I knew that Lestrade would do the same, as duty required him to.

I looked again at the lifeless body of Inspector Forbes. Except for the faint but growing tinge of blue, he looked the picture of robust good health. His complexion was as if he had just stepped in from an hour of standing out in the cold, had entered the room, laid down on the floor, and given up the ghost.

"How did he get in here," I asked, "if both exterior doors and the one to this room were locked?"

Both Holmes and Lestrade gave me a condescending look.

"I suppose," I hastened to add, "that someone could have picked the locks."

"I could name twenty men," said Lestrade, "who could have opened both doors in minutes."

"How true," agreed Holmes. "But please tell me, Inspector, did he have his notebook on his person?"

"He did. I have it here. I'll leave it with you. But there was nothing in it that was helpful. Last entry was yesterday afternoon when he sorted out some minor squabble between fishmongers."

"He did, I presume, leave a note at the dispatch desk as to his expected destination?"

"I expect he did," said Lestrade. "Perhaps Inspector Jones can ask about it when he gets back to the Yard. Now, if you will excuse me, I have to go and speak to his family."

Inspector Lestrade walked slowly out of the room and back down the hall. He did not look well.

Holmes turned to Inspector Jones. "Now then, sir, do you know when Forbes was last seen? Did he stop in at the Yard this morning? Was he out and about on any other assignment earlier this morning?"

"Well now, that is a peculiar matter," said Jones. "He was not seen anywhere this morning as far as I know. Last time he was seen anywhere was last night at the Langham Hotel."

"Why!" I sputtered. "That was with me. We walked back together after the reception. I said goodnight to him on the corner of Marylebone and Baker Street."

"Yes, Doctor," said Jones. "You were the last person to see him alive that we can account for. Would you mind telling me why you were with him?"

Chapter Two
Attacked in the Press

The previous evening had been a splendid affair, not just because it was a posh reception at one of London's finest hotels, but because I, Dr. John H. Watson, had been the guest of honor.

The delightful event was the annual dinner of the British Medical Association. Being doctors, they are always looking for some fresh ways to remind the populace that the profession of medicine is to be revered and respected beyond all others. Thus, they are constantly on the lookout for yet another member of our club who could be feted for selfless rushing out on a snowy night to deliver a baby, or a handsome, heroic young army medic fresh from the battlefield, or the latest brilliant researcher who had discovered a miraculous cure for a dreaded disease. They had, in some desperation I expected, decided that my humble exploits in accompanying the famous detective, Sherlock Holmes, and in helping him in some small ways to solve no end of heinous crimes, merited a citation of sorts. The Strand magazine had made a sizeable contribution to the evening and had several of their staff present so that they could take the names and addresses of all who attended and subscribe them free for three monthly issues, after which they would have to pay the full fare.

And so, I had been honored and toasted and given a small plaque as "a token of our esteem." To me, it seemed rather a bit much, but Mary was thrilled. Holmes, as would be expected, did not attend, but several officers of Scotland Yard had been invited to add a touch of drama for the benefit of the Press.

At the end of the evening, my wife and I left the hotel and, it being a perfectly still, deep winter night with the stars shining in their vast heavenly display, we decided to walk back to our home near Paddington. Inspector Forbes bumped into us as we departed the hotel and joined us for the stroll. When we reached the corner of Baker Street, he bade us goodnight and, saying that he had some police business to attend to, turned and proceeded along Baker Street. Whatever happened between that time and the discovery of his body was entirely unknown.

"Why were we with him?" I said to Jones. "There was no particular reason. We met by happenstance as we were leaving and we chatted and agreed that it was a jolly good night for a stroll and the three of us walked together."

"Indeed," said the inspector. "And what did you talk about? It is a good twenty minutes from the Langham to the corner of Baker Street. Did Forbes want to know something? Did he ask you anything? What was discussed?"

I wracked my memory.

"Nothing."

"Nothing?" persisted Jones. "You do not chat for twenty minutes about nothing. There must have been something."

"Good Lord," I exclaimed. "Of course, we talked about something, but nothing of any significance."

"Well, such as?"

"Oh goodness. We chatted about the lovely starry night, and about how we had spent Christmas, and all that. And yes, he did ask how Holmes was getting along. He thinks quite highly of him."

"And that was all? All friendly like? No harsh words?"

"Of course not. I did not know the man well, but there was never so much as a hint of animosity between us."

"No, perhaps not. But you did make him look bad in that story you wrote about a case he was involved in."

"Oh, come now," I said. "That was years ago."

It was true that in my account of the missing naval treaty I might have presented the police officer as a bit of a numbskull, but there was no malice intended.

"So, you did not have any words at all between you."

"No. None at all. Besides, I was with my wife, and Inspector Forbes is, or at least was, enough of a gentleman that even if he did hold a grudge against me all these years later, he would never voice it in front of my wife."

"Hmm. Yes. Well, if you say so."

"Good heavens! You are not suggesting that I had anything to do with his death, are you?"

"Oh, no. No. Not at all. Just trying to gather up all the pieces and put them together. That is what we professional detectives have to do even after all these years of watching Holmes do otherwise. It was necessary to confirm that you were the last man to see him alive."

"Other than whoever killed him," I said, in a manner more forceful than I am accustomed to using.

"Right. Yes. Of course. Other than person or persons unknown, who appear to be clever enough to kill a strong, healthy policeman without leaving a mark."

I did not like the tone of this conversation and was about to give Inspector Jones a piece of my mind when Holmes graciously intervened.

"Was there anything, Inspector, that connected Forbes to me? He was, after all, found on Baker Street directly across the road from my home."

"Right. Well, that is a good question, Mr. Holmes. I do not know of anything at the moment, but I shall be looking into it. Now if you will excuse me, I have to return to the Yard and continue my investigation into this case."

He turned and departed, leaving Holmes and me in the small back room along with the corpse of Inspector Forbes and a constable who had been posted there.

"Are you," I asked Holmes, "going to inspect the rest of the house?"

"No. The site has been quite disturbed, but the marks on the floor indicate that he was dragged by one man through the back door and deposited in the place he now rests. The scuffs from his heels and the marks of one man walking backward are still discernible. Had items been disturbed in the other rooms of the house, Lestrade's men would have informed him."

"Anything else?" I asked.

"Only one thing, and I cannot make any sense of it. If you look at the floor in the doorway to this room, it appears to have been wiped or dusted. I am sure that it has some significance, but as of yet, I cannot decide what."

I looked at the spot he had referred to but could make no sense of it either. As there was nothing more to discuss, Holmes and I returned to 221B across the street.

"I found," I said after we had left the empty house, "Jones highly annoying."

"He was just doing his duty," answered Holmes. "And I am aware that he and Forbes were quite close and worked together on many cases. Rather like you and me, my friend. He was doing a good job of keeping the stiff upper lip, but I suspect that inwardly, he was in great turmoil. And when men are in that disposition, they tend to forget their social graces. It is nothing to worry about. But come now, let me offer you a brandy by the fire so you can still your soul before returning to your home. If I am not mistaken, your good wife should have returned by now and will be waiting for you."

He was right, so I quaffed my brandy quickly and made my way out into the dark, winter night. I left Holmes to ponder over the reasons that a murder of a Scotland Yard inspector had happened immediately across the road from 221B Baker Street. Somewhere along Marylebone Road, it dawned on me that I had forgotten completely about our dear departed Queen.

By the time I returned home, my dinner was cold, and my dear wife was none too pleased with me.

I hastened to explain my tardiness, and she graciously sat and had a cup of tea with me whilst I struggled through a plate of now dried out lamb chops, during which time I recounted to my wife the events of the past several hours.

"And so," she mused, "you and Sherlock both believe that it was some unknown poison?"

"That is the best hypothesis so far," I said.

"That is rather curious, you know."

"Really, darling? In what way?"

"Sherlock Holmes solved another case that started out at the Langham Hotel and ended with murder by strange poison."

He did?" I queried and searched my memory. "Which case was that?"

"Mine, dear husband. Mine"

"Oh ... yes ... of course."

I heard nothing from Holmes for the next two days, and I busied myself with attending to my patients and catching up on reading the medical journals. Then, early on the third morning, before we had even gotten out of bed, my wife awakened me with a friendly kick to my lower leg.

"Darling, there is something going on outside our door. Listen."

I shook the slumber from my brain and became aware of voices coming through our front door. I got up and peeked through the curtains and observed in the early morning light a score of men gathered on the pavement in front of our home. They were all dressed somewhat carelessly in trench coats that did not appear to be keeping them warm on a cold January morning. Most were puffing on cigarettes, and all were clutching either notebooks or cameras.

"The Press," I said. "What in heaven's name are they doing here?"

"Well darling," answered my wife, "they must be waiting for either you or me to emerge, and I suspect that it is not me."

"Should I go out and see what they want?"

"No darling, you should bathe, dress and have your breakfast and then depart at your usual time."

"They won't be very happy having to wait there in the cold," I said.

"Good. And if half of them caught pneumonia and died, would the world be any the worse?"

"Quite so. Let us enjoy a leisurely breakfast."

Throughout our breakfast there came several knocks on our door and persistent ringing of our bell. We ignored all of them, but I must admit that my curiosity was getting the better of me. I gulped down my last swallow of tea and went to the front hall closet to pull on my coat.

"Not that coat," said my wife. "It is cold outside. You need your warm winter coat. You do not want to appear to be shivering whilst they are taking your picture."

Warmly clad in my heavy woolen coat, scarf, gloves, and hat, I ventured out into the late January morning. I had no sooner opened the door than a young reporter bounded up my stairs.

"Good morning, Dr. Watson. Mind if we ask you a few questions, and how about being a friendly chap and letting us come inside to do so?"

I ignored the impertinence, pulled the door closed behind me and descended into the gaggle. Several flashes of powder from cameras exploded in front of me, followed immediately by a cacophony of shouted questions.

"Dr. Watson! Is it true that you were the last person to see Inspector Forbes alive?"

"What? No, that is not true."

"Do you deny seeing him after your reception at the Langham?" came from another reporter.

"No. I did not say that?"

"Why did he demand to have a word with you?" Now a third man had chimed in.

"He did no such thing."

"So, you deny talking to him."

"I did not say that," I said, now shouting in return.

"You just said that he did not talk to you."

"I said no such thing," I replied, now more than somewhat annoyed.

"Did he inform you that you were being investigated? Maybe sued for slander?"

"Good heavens, no. What possible reason would he have for doing that?"

"Did he tell you that he had evidence that your citation was fraudulent?"

"That is nonsense. He said nothing of the kind."

"So, you now admit that he did demand to speak to you. What did he accuse you of?"

"Nothing," I shouted, now quite angry.

"Nobody talks about nothing. What did he have on you? Did it make you angry? Angry enough for you to want to get rid of him?"

I could not believe what I was hearing from this pack of unruly hyenas and walked briskly along the pavement in search of a cab. The swarm of reporters dogged my footsteps, keeping up their highly offensive questions. Finally, I hailed a cab and reflexively gave them Holmes's address.

I was upset beyond words as I raced up the steps at 221B and barged into the front room. Holmes was dressed in his blue dressing gown, pacing the floor and puffing on a cigarette. I blurted my outrage. He said nothing in response and merely gestured for me to take a seat across from him.

"Well!" I demanded. "Are you not going to tell me how to make this vile nonsense cease and desist? It was unbearable. I have never been so egregiously insulted in my life!"

He puffed several more times.

"My dear friend," he said. "I am terribly sorry for what you had to endure, and, quite possibly, you have not seen the end of it. However, the fact that it happened is of singular interest."

"What can you possibly mean by that?"

"What I mean is that someone obviously slipped the information to the Press, else how could they have known?

Prior to this moment, the only people who were aware that you chatted with Forbes late that evening are yourself, your good wife, myself, and Inspectors Lestrade and Jones. I am quite certain that none of the above said anything to any member of the Press. There must have been someone else who not only attended the reception but followed you to Baker Street. Whoever it was is may be involved in the murder of Forbes."

"But why send lies about me to the Press?"

Holmes paused and puffed some more. "Whoever it was knows the Press well enough to assume that they will print anything regardless if it is true or false as long as it makes a sensational headline and promotes sales. If they did that, it is quite possible that their motive was not merely the death of Forbes. They may be angry at all of Scotland Yard and, given the location of the crime, at me as well. He may be seeking to wreak revenge not merely by murder but by raining humiliation on all of us. Ah, yes. It was very instructive of them to invoke the scandal mongers of the Press."

"But why me?"

"It was not about you. It was about me. You are my dear friend and my Boswell. Mark my words, Watson. Whatever they say about you, false and distorted though it may be, will be sure to include a reminder of our splendid friendship. And the murder of a Scotland Yard inspector almost on my doorstep will cast aspersions not only on me but on Scotland Yard. Yes ... yes ... whoever it is, is starting to show his hand. How terribly foolish of him. But I should not worry, Watson, within a few days I suspect that you shall be all but forgotten and that I shall become the target. That is quite useful. An angry man seeking revenge makes for a very poor criminal."

I had half expected that he would begin rubbing his hands together in expectation as he often did. Instead, his fists were clenched, and his knuckles had whitened.

Chapter Three
A Rothschild in 220 Baker Street

I took a cab back to my medical practice and managed, with great efforts of concentration, to give my attention to my patients. At the end of the day, I departed my office and picked up an afternoon copy of *The Evening Star* on the way home. As expected, I was on the front page. There was a picture of me appearing to be running away from the reporters. The headline read 'Famous Doctor Friend of Sherlock Holmes Refuses to Answer Questions.' The story began with the self-serving words 'On a freezing cold morning, our reporter waited outside a lavish home in the posh neighborhood of Little Venice for Dr. John H. Watson, the 'partner-in-crime' of Sherlock Holmes, to appear.' It went on to quote 'reliable sources' who had revealed that I was 'the last known person to see Inspector Forbes alive' and therefore might be a suspect in his murder. The paper ever went so far as to print a photo of the inspector's wife and children in distress on receiving the awful news of the death of their 'dear Daddy.' And, as Holmes had predicted, the location of the crime 'on the doorstep of Sherlock Holmes, possibly whilst he was napping' was repeated in various ways throughout the story.

I was furious at the duplicity of the Press, and even the kind ministrations of my wife failed to soothe my righteous indignation. I slept little and got up the next morning ready to give the gang of blighters a piece of my mind, but when I opened the door, there was not a single reporter in sight. As Holmes had also predicted, they had moved on. I was yesterday's news.

My day passed uneventfully, and I was happy that my waiting room had emptied by just after three o'clock. For reasons that I cannot truly explain, but that were no doubt tied to the disconcerting happenings of the previous day, I was anxious to speak again with Holmes. I caught a cab and directed the driver to Baker Street, but as soon as we turned off Marylebone, I looked up the road and could see the pack of pests from the Press now gathered on the pavement outside of 221B. Holmes was right. They were now out to sell more papers by disgracing his good name.

I told the driver to pass by the address and come back up the alley that lay behind that stretch of Baker Street. Once we reached the back door of 221, I stepped out of the cab and knocked on the back door. A very distraught Mrs. Hudson greeted me. She was holding a rolling pin in her hand.

"Oh, Doctor," she gasped when she saw me. "I am so glad it is you. If one more of those vermin had pounded on my door, I was ready to let him have it."

I had never before suspected the good woman of contemplating violence, but she looked ready to do battle. I tried to calm her with assurances that, just as in my case, the hounds would depart once they were attracted to a new scent.

Holmes was sitting again at the table, again smoking a cigarette, but this time poring over a stack of papers that, from a distance, appeared to be a list of names and addresses.

"Watson, good to see you," he said in a manner that betrayed his calm state, entirely untouched by the raving rabble outside the door. "I could have used your help earlier today. It would have made matters much more efficient, but I did somehow manage to get by eventually on my own."

That piqued my curiosity. "What were you up to?"

"I dropped in at Number 12 Burleigh Street. They are very fond of you there."

"The office of the *Strand*? Whatever for?"

The Strand had been publishing my stories about the adventures of Sherlock Holmes for over fifteen years and was wonderfully grateful to me for the way their sales and subscriptions soared every time a new story about Holmes appeared. Although modesty forbade me to boast about it, I had to admit that I was one of their favorite people in all of London. I was always greeted as next of kin to royalty every time I entered their premises.

"You had a fine reception a few days back to which they made a generous donation."

"Yes, Holmes. I am aware of that. I was there, and you did not attend. Remember?"

"Quite so. But you did happen to mention that they offered free subscriptions to all those who attended and paid the exorbitant entrance fee that was tantamount to robbery."

"It all went to a good cause, The British Medical Association," I said.

"Ah yes, of course, to give aid and succor to all the underfed, underpaid, and terribly put-upon doctors. The rents those poor dears are charged for their suites on Harley Street are miserably unfair. But questioning the righteousness of the cause was not my purpose. I wanted a copy of the list of all those who signed up for the free subscription. At first, they were not willing to give it to me, citing proprietary assets, privacy and the like. I had to suggest that their failure to cooperate might result in my refusing to have you accompany me on any more of our adventures, thus bringing to a halt yet again their glorious and highly profitable publishing of your sensational accounts of my investigations. It was a bit heavy-handed of me, but time was of the essence, and the threat worked wonderfully."

I was about to express my outrage at the gall of Holmes's threatening my publisher, but he called me over to look at the lists.

"You attracted quite that interesting audience; I must say," he said. "Look here. There is a fine assortment of blue-bloods, captains of industry, bankers, writers, publishers, actors ... even a clergyman or two. Well done."

"Thank you, Holmes. But what is the purpose of your wanting the list."

"Elementary, my dear Watson. It is highly probable that whoever murdered Inspector Forbes and subsequently slipped the details of your walk home with him to the Press must have been present at your reception and followed you."

"Fine. I agree. But there was over a hundred people there. You cannot investigate every one of them."

"An excellent conclusion, Watson. But I can quickly remove all those who I know to be upright citizens and beyond reproach. And then I can look for names and addresses that seem incongruous with such an event."

"Very well. Did you find any?"

"Oh, there were at least twenty that I either had never heard of or that I recognized and knew to run rather close to the law. But take a look at the name I have circled. Do you recognize it?"

He handed me the sheets of paper. On the fourth page, I read the name he had circled:

Lionel Walter Rothschild

"Good heavens!" I exclaimed. "I had no idea I had attracted one of the wealthiest men in the Empire."

"My dear Watson," said Holmes, condescension dripping from his voice. "You had no idea because he most certainly did not attend. Kindly look at the address given for the complimentary subscription to the Strand magazine."

I looked again, and again I was startled.

"Why, he gives an address of 220 Baker Street. That is just across the street from here."

"Precisely, and I assure you that the Baron Rothschild does not live in Mrs. Turner's boarding house and nor is he likely to need to take advantage of a free magazine subscription regardless of where he lives."

"That does appear to be very odd," I said.

"Precisely, now Watson, does that not also strike you as suspicious?"

"Most assuredly. We should send a note off to Inspector Lestrade this instant and have the whole lot of people living there brought in."

"Not so quickly, my dear doctor. I am inclined to suspect that one of them may be a murderer or at least connected to the crime, but if we reveal our hand too soon, we have nothing with which to charge and hold him, and he would be back on the streets in minutes. If I am correct in my suspicions, he or, we must bear in mind, possibly *she*, would disappear from London before morning. I think it best that we continue our investigation and come up with more evidence before making our move."

"And just how are you going to do that?"

"With the help of our dear landlady."

He stood up quickly and walked to the door and called for Mrs. Hudson. She appeared in less than a minute.

"Yes, Mr. Holmes. Is there something you need?" she said.

"I need you to help me solve a case."

She smiled involuntarily. "Oh, well, if you think there is some little thing I could do, I would be happy to oblige."

"Not a little thing, Mrs. Hudson. Possibly a very big thing. It has to do with the murder of Inspector Forbes."

Her eyes widened, and she gasped. "Oh, my. Why, that was awful, and to think it happened right across the road from our home here. Let me tell you, Mr. Holmes, the whole neighborhood has been talking about nothing since."

"Have they now? Asked Holmes. "And what have they been saying."

"Oh, you know, Mr. Holmes. All about how terrible it was and how we all thought our street was safe, and how everyone needs to lock their doors all the time now because you never know who is out there. Just the things that you would expect."

"Of course, but allow me to be more specific. What have they been saying about me?"

"About you, Mr. Holmes?"

"Yes, Mrs. Hudson, about me? And please, the truth and the whole truth."

The poor woman blushed and looked very uncomfortable.

"Well, Mr. Holmes, if you must know …"

"Yes, Mrs. Hudson, I must."

"Very well, Mr. Holmes. Before the terrible murder of the police inspector, all of the neighbors were quite proud to share the street with London's most famous detective. But now, and I am not sure how to say this, now they would rather you found somewhere else to live. What with the murder, and the nasty things in the paper about Dr. Watson, and the swarm of reporters on the street all morning. It has made them all quite distressed."

"They have my sympathies. I cannot blame them. But what about your friend across the street, Mrs. Turner. Does she feel that way as well?

Mrs. Hudson gave Holmes a bit of a look.

"It is odd that you ask about her, but I suppose I might have expected it, coming from you. I did have a chat with Mrs. Turner just an hour ago. She was quite strong in her condemnation of all the gossip and sang your praises, saying how fortunate we all were in times of trial to have a famous detective as a neighbor looking out for us. As far as she was concerned, it made the entire street safer."

"That was very kind of her," said Holmes. "Please remember to pass along my appreciation for her thoughts."

"Well, if you must know, Mr. Holmes. Those thoughts were not truly hers. She said that, at first, she was inclined to agree with the rest of the neighbors and, being my friend and all, she had a duty to let me know how she felt about you living here and all. But then she said something about it to the boarders living in her house and didn't they give her something to think about. They must be quite your fans Mr. Holmes. They would not hear any talk about telling you to move. No, they were the ones that made it clear to Mrs. Turner that they did not want you to leave Baker Street. No, not one bit. As a matter of fact, if you must know, they said that you're being here was one of the reasons they chose this street to live on. They feel good and safe knowing that you are right across the road from them and had members of Scotland Yard always coming and going."

"Ah, well, they must be quite the fine lot of boarders, wouldn't you say, Mrs. Hudson?"

Again, she gave Holmes a bit of a look before answering.

"Well now Mr. Holmes, I do not know that I would quite say that."

"Indeed? And why not?"

"Well, if you must know, Mr. Holmes, they are the oddest lot of boarders I ever laid my eyes on. Odd indeed, that's what they are."

"You don't say. Please, Mrs. Hudson, I am intrigued. Why would you say that?"

The good woman hesitated before answering. "Mr. Holmes, it is not a good Christian thing to speak ill of anyone behind his back."

"Of course not, Mrs. Hudson. It is not at all. But as part of the investigation into the tragic death of Inspector Forbes, it is simply a matter of course that we learn everything we can about everyone in the neighborhood where the crime occurred. I do believe that the Holy Scriptures instruct us to obey the laws and give honor and obedience to those in authority over us."

"Oh, yes, well, if you say so. I suppose it would not be improper then if I were just to say that they were odd. Being odd is no sin. The way they all came to Mrs. Turner in the past four months was the first odd thing. She keeps a fine house and has always had her rooms full, but starting four months ago the toff, the aristocrat chap, came to her door and said he wanted to rent a room, and she said that she had none to let and he said that he would pay her twice the rate she was receiving and pay it all up front for a full year. Well, that is a situation that a landlady cannot afford to say no to and I will have to be honest, Mr. Holmes, if he had come here and made the same offer, I would be hard-pressed not to send you packing and take him in instead. No offense intended, Mr. Holmes."

"And none taken. It would be a practical business decision. Pray continue."

"Well, if you must know, she gave notice to one of her boarders and sent him off even though he had done nothing amiss. But, and here's where it gets very odd, Mr. Holmes, over the next month don't two of her boarders suddenly up and leave, and another two show up. And then two more all come to her door and make her the same offer and say they are willing to pay much more than what she has been receiving. They're all saying that they want to live on Baker Street not just because of the Underground nearby but because it is a famous street on account of Mr. Sherlock Holmes living here, and it is something they can brag about to their families wherever they might be as they have all heard of Baker Street from the stories written by Dr. Watson. So, Mrs. Turner gave notice to all the last two of her old boarders and has a whole new lot of them, and near twice the income she had expected for the year. As far as she is concerned, and I cannot blame her one little bit, the lot of them can be as odd as they want seeing as their money is not only good but twice as good as what she was getting before. Now that is quite all I know, Mr. Holmes. If you must know anything more, you'll have to ask her yourself."

Holmes nodded and smiled warmly at the dear lady. "You have been exceptionally helpful, Mrs. Hudson. I do not know what I would do without you. But I need to beg your indulgence and ask you to help me with one more thing."

"If it is something I can do, then it is something I will do, Mr. Holmes."

"Would you be so kind as to ask your friend, Mrs. Turner, over for early tea tomorrow? And try to do it on very short notice, and do not mention that Dr. Watson and I will be present. Now, I am not asking you to lie to her, just not to voluntarily reveal anything about our interest in her and her boarders. Would you mind doing that for me, Mrs. Hudson?"

The lady looked quite puzzled but gave her assent. However, she did give Holmes a long, queer look as she departed from our room.

I bade Holmes goodbye, promised to return the following day at the same time and made my way home in time for supper.

Chapter Four
Quite the Rum Lot

I returned the next day as I had agreed and found Holmes pacing back and forth with a cigarette in hand. His appearance and manner betrayed a soul seething with barely controlled anger. He ignored me and kept pacing and appeared to be rehearsing his lines for a performance on stage. After observing him for several minutes, I took advantage of a short pause when he reached the far wall and had to turn around.

"Would you mind terribly, Holmes," I said, "stopping whatever it is you are doing long enough to say 'hello' and tell me what is about to happen, seeing as I have come over to try to assist you?"

"Oh, yes, of course, Watson," he said, coming back to his usual congenial self. "Mrs. Hudson, bless her, has gone over to invite Mrs. Turner to tea. Both of them should be back here in five minutes. I have to find a way to have Mrs. Turner tell me all she knows about her current boarders without alarming her or rushing back to tell the lot of them that I am making inquiries."

"Very well, do you have to ask about every one of them? Do you believe they all murdered Forbes?"

"No, of course not. But it is highly likely that at least one of them is tied to the crime. However, as I do not have near sufficient data to lead me to know which one that might be, I have no choice but to ask about all of them."

I thought for a moment and then offered the advice given to all men in the medical profession.

"Then just tell her the truth. Be completely candid. No varnishing or sugar-coating allowed. Tell her that one or more of her boarders might possibly be connected to the murder that took place next door to her and that you need her help to identify that person. Or, if you are mistaken, clear all of their names so that Scotland Yard will not be investigating her entire house, and possibly herself."

"I cannot see how that would encourage her to want to assist me. She is thrilled to have lodgers who have paid twice the going rent and given it a year in advance."

"Then point out to her that if any one, or two, or even three are taken into custody and sent away, she can just go right ahead and rent out the rooms one more time. She will end up with thrice the income."

Holmes glared at me as if I had just landed from an unknown planet.

"Watson ... that is brilliant. Forgive me for underestimating your business acumen."

"Must I remind you, Holmes, that I am by heritage a Scotsman. Some matters concerning money are in the blood."

For the next few minutes, Holmes and I rehearsed our lines and plotted how we would gently coerce Mrs. Turner into giving up all she knew about her boarders. Holmes insisted that I should take the lead, reminding me that the fair sex was my department.

The two ladies arrived with Mrs. Hudson leading the way. Her friend, Mrs. Turner, was well-known to both Holmes and me as she had on numerous occasions over the years stood in for Mrs. Hudson when family matters took our landlady away for a spell. I had first met her years ago at the time Holmes had been engaged by the King of Bohemia and she had prepared our dinner in Mrs. Hudson's absence. We stood and greeted the two of them when they entered.

"Oh. Why it's Mr. Holmes and Dr. Watson," exclaimed Mrs. Turner as she entered. "Martha did not tell me that both of you were in. Oh, I am so glad that you are here. I have been praying that God would help me out of the terrible quandary I am in, and He has sent you."

I was not prepared to have divine provision accorded to us, but I smiled and extended a friendly greeting in return.

"My dear Mrs. Turner," I said. "Please, relax yourself, have a cup of tea and tell us all about your quandary."

I fully expected that she was about to launch into her latest scrap with the gas man and I hoped that we could dispose of it before enticing her to reveal all we needed to know about her boarders.

"It's my boarders," she said. "I do not know what to do about them and, frankly, I have become quite fearful."

My surprise was overtaken by my amusement, concealed of course, at seeing Holmes react as if someone had sent a jolt of electricity through the chair he was sitting on.

"Is that so?" he said. "Why then, by all means, let us hear about it. As your friends and neighbors, we have an obligation to do whatever we can to help."

"Oh, thank you, Mr. Holmes, but I was worried that your fee would be far beyond my means seeing as you have become so famous and in demand by all the nobility and royals and what not."

"My dear Mrs. Turner," Holmes replied. "There will be no fee whatsoever charged. The good Lord commanded us to love our neighbor as ourselves, and you are our closest neighbor. So, consider any assistance I can provide to be a labor of love and moral obligation. All other cases will be put aside, and yours will have precedence. Please, tell us about your situation and hold nothing back. You have my complete attention."

I took out my notebook and pencil and prepared to record a wonderfully uncoerced account.

"Well, Mr. Holmes. I do not know if Martha, Mrs. Hudson I mean, has told you, but over the past four months I have taken in an entire new set of boarders."

"I had," said Holmes, "noticed that myself. There has been a new set of faces coming and going from 220 Baker Street this season. Are they freeloading and refusing to pay their rents?"

"Oh no, not at all. Every one of them, all five of them that is, has paid an entire year in advance at a higher rate than I had been receiving last year. Oh no, the matter has nothing to do with money, Mr. Holmes."

"Ah, well that is good news," said Holmes. "Then what is the issue? Are they engaging in illegal activities? Gambling? Immoral liaisons? Wild debauched parties?"

"Oh no, nothing like that. They are quite clean living, every one of them. Mind you, none of them, not one, appears to be gainfully employed. They come and go at all hours during the day, but they do not appear to be short of funds. No, not at all. Oh, I am going to sound like a foolish old woman saying this, but I have become afraid of them. They insisted on paying all that rent and handed me envelopes filled with notes. Not one offered a check on their bank accounts. I usually demand a letter from a tenant's previous landlord but they all claimed that they had either been abroad, or had owned property themselves, or some such excuse and as they paid a year in advance, I wasn't concerned about their probity."

"Yes. That is unusual. Pray, keep going," said Holmes.

"I began to suspect that perhaps one or two of them might be using a false name, an alias, and maybe on the run from the law or creditors. Several times I heard them address each other by names other than the ones they had given me."

"Ah, did you now? That is a good cause for suspicion."

"Well, I did something that I fear I might regret for the rest of my life. Three weeks ago, I told my doctor about my fears. I believe you know Dr. Trevelyan down on Brook Street. Well, he was very kind — he always is — and he suggested that I come and speak to you, especially as you are my neighbor here on Baker Street. I told him that I was in no position to pay for such services and he then suggested that I have a chat with Inspector Forbes at Scotland Yard, who he knew as well, and he offered to arrange a meeting with the inspector. Well, I did have that chat and, at first, I thought the inspector considered me a silly old widow but as I told him about my suspicions he became very interested. He took down notes and asked me all sorts of questions, and two days later he paid a visit to my house on the pretense of being concerned about vagrants in the empty house next door, Camden House they call it, but of course you know that. He wanted to have a chat with each of the tenants to see if they had heard of anything untoward happening and make sure that the neighborhood was safe. So, he did that — quite clever he was at chatting with them — and in doing so he asked for their names and some questions about their identity. And he took down everything they said. Now, I was not in his presence whilst he was doing that, so I did not hear what all they said.

Well, I might have overheard one or two things, but that was all."

"Ah, but you remember those things that you did hear, do you not?" asked Holmes.

"Oh yes, mind you they are not of much use to anyone for it seems that everything they said was made up."

"Indeed? And how do you know that?"

"Well, a week later, Inspector Forbes comes by again and first he takes me aside and tells me to be very careful. It seems he had checked out all the stories he had been given by my boarders and not one of them was true. He said, and he was quite sharp on this, that I should take precautions because he suspected that the lot of them were up to no good. And I should be careful to lock my bedroom door at night, and not go out into the back alley behind the house alone, and especially not at night. And then after he talks to me he takes each of the boarders into the parlor alone and has a chat with them."

"Yes, and did you happen to overhear any of those conversations?" asked Holmes.

"No. Not a word. But each of them, all five of the boarders that is, comes out of the meeting and has quite the dark look on his face, or her face when it was one of the two women. I could tell that after their meeting the four who were not having a chat with the inspector were gathered in one of the bedrooms and having quite the chin-wag amongst themselves."

"An excellent observation," said Holmes. "That is quite significant. Now, what can you tell me about the boarders themselves?"

"Oh, they are quite the motley crew, they are. The second chap who came by says that he is a doctor, Dr. Govinda Roulston he says he is. He's from India all right. No arguing that. Brown skin, black hair and all. Mind you he is awfully big for an Indian. Most of those chaps are scrawny, the runt of the litter if you know what I mean, but not the doctor. No, he's a big one he is. As tall as you, Mr. Holmes and as thick as Dr. Watson here. I would not be surprised if his father were not an Indian at all, but one of our big soldiers who served under the Raj. So many of those boys went native, as they say, which is to be expected, boys being boys as they will be."

"And is he," I asked, "treating patients? Or associated with any hospital?"

"No. Not yet, he says. Just recently come from Calcutta and waiting to get his papers, he says. After that, he will be a right legal doctor."

"Interesting," acknowledged Holmes. "And the next one to register with you? Who was that?"

"That was Miss Alwyn Owen. As you can guess from her name, she's as Welsh as the day is long. She says she is a 'Miss,' but she is no spring chicken. She's about your age, Mr. Holmes. She says that she has spent her life in service but when her last master died she was left a bit in his will, and now she wants to live in London. Nice enough, lass. Friendly and talkative as you might expect from the Welsh and seems a bit overfond of the gentlemen folk. A bit of a temper too, mind you, but again that is to be expected from those who grew up in those wild hills. Now the very first fellow to come by, well, he is a conundrum if ever there was one."

"Is he now? In what way?"

"He says his name is John Clarke, which is about as common a name as you can imagine. But heavens, if he does not strut around like he is Prince Bertie. All manners and posh he is. Dressed to the nines all the time. I overheard him once remind the others that he had royal blood in his veins and didn't the lot of them start calling him Little Lord Fauntleroy. Not to his face, mind you. And what surprises me is why he would want to live in a boarding house. The man is not without means. He drinks fine claret and sends his clothing out once a week to the laundry service. And he even owns a motor car. He keeps it parked behind the house and every Saturday he takes it out for a jolly run through the country. Not so much now that the winter has set in, but come spring, he will be off and running again; I would wager."

"A curious fellow, I must say," mused Holmes. "There are two more. Yes?"

"Oh, yes. The German girl. Fräulein Gretta; Greta Schmidt. Now she is quite the piece of work, she is. Young and beautiful. Takes a man's breath away she does. As tall as you, Mr. Holmes. Blonde hair, blue eyes. Walks as if she had a ramrod for a spine. If you ever wondered what Princess Brunhilde looked like, well, that's her. Not friendly though. Not in the least. Just about as aloof and arrogant as they come, and again I cannot imagine why she is living in a boarding house on Baker Street. She should be married to some kraut Count or mistress to the Kaiser; she should."

Holmes was clearly fascinated by the accounts of the boarders across the street. He kept nodding and had begun to rub his hands together.

"And the last one, Mrs. Hudson. Tell me about the final fellow."

"Mr. Tarker, yes. Well, he is the smallest of the lot. Smaller even than the Welsh woman. But bless me if he is not the most frightening of the bunch. He has those dark eyes that are always darting back and forth. He walks without making a sound. Hardly ever says a word. But I swear if he had it in for you, he would cut your throat as soon as look at you. I do not know anything more about him, so I cannot say any more. So, that's the whole of them, Mr. Holmes. Is there anything else I can tell you? I really cannot think of anything else, but if there is, sir, just let me know."

Holmes smiled and nodded and then closed his eyes. For the next minute, his lips moved almost imperceptibly and his head alternated between small nods and shakes. Poor Mrs. Turner looked at him as if gazing at some alien being. Mrs. Hudson reached her hand over and patted the wrist of her friend and mouthed some words of reassurance, then held up her hand to signal 'just be patient.'

Having observed Holmes in this type of behavior before, I was fully expecting that in a few seconds he would open his eyes, smile, and pronounce his verdict.

I was wrong.

Suddenly we were interrupted by a terrific pounding on the door to Baker Street, accompanied by a non-ceasing ringing of the bell. Mrs. Hudson leapt to her feet and scampered down the stairs. I heard the door open and then a familiar voice, louder than I had ever heard it before.

"HOLMES! HOLMES!" Inspector Lestrade was screaming. "Holmes get down here! Now! NOW!"

I jumped up and rushed down the stairs with Holmes on my heels.

"What is it?" I shouted.

Lestrade was already out of the door and part way across Baker Street by the time we were on the pavement.

"This way!" he shouted. He ran across the street and around a police wagon that was parked on the far side.

We followed him into the open door of Camden House. There were several constables standing in the entryway, all with grave faces.

"Back here," called Lestrade. "Same room."

We hustled our way through the kitchen and into the room we had first seen a week earlier. On the floor, in the same position as Inspector Forbes had been before, was the body of a man. He was clad in a similar heavy trench coat, woolen trousers, and police boots as Forbes had been.

"It's ... it's Jones. It's Jones," said Lestrade, his voice almost inaudible and trembling.

Holmes and I, stunned, stood speechless for a respectful moment before Holmes quietly spoke to Lestrade.

"Everything the same as last week?"

Lestrade nodded took in a deep breath and answered. "Everything. The estate agent checked in an hour ago. The doors were all locked. Nothing else disturbed. No one, neither in the back or on Baker Street, reported seeing anyone enter the house all day."

Holmes was silent.

Lestrade turned to me, his face white as chalk. "Doctor, would you please pronounce again?"

I got down on my hands and knees and began again to examine the body. Once again there were no signs of any struggle; no cuts; no swellings. His face was flushed and healthy looking. Rigor mortis was beginning to set in, and there was a bluish tinge to the eyelids, lips and neck, and just the beginning of discoloring and stiffening to the limbs.

"The exact same as before," I said. "He has been dead anywhere from five to eight hours. Again, I suspect some sort of poison, but all the usual concoctions are ruled out."

I stood up slowly, and the three of us remained still for another minute without speaking before Lestrade broke the silence.

"There was one peculiar thing this time around."

"Yes," said Holmes. "And what was that?"

"His notebook. It was all quite the usual, except that there was a folded page that he had inserted into it."

"All it had on it was 'Sherlock Holmes. 220 Baker Street."

"220?" I said. "Surely he knew where Holmes lived."

"It was not Jones's handwriting," said Lestrade. "It was Forbes's. And I am quite certain he knew where you lived as well. Thanks to you, Dr. Watson, your address has become the most famous in London outside of Buckingham Palace."

"I suspect it was no mistake," said Holmes. "And, I beg your forgiveness, my dear Inspector. I should have seen this coming. I shall take steps tomorrow morning and, Lord willing, this will all come to a stop."

"Please, Holmes, do whatever you have to do, and I do not care how you do it, lawful or otherwise. And now, if you will excuse me, I have to go and take the news to Mrs. Jones and her children."

He walked slowly out of the room and down the hall. He demeanor was like that of a man who wished he were dead.

I followed Holmes out of Camden House and onto the pavement of Baker Street. He stopped and lit a cigarette. Neither of us had taken the time to pull on our overcoats before answering Lestrade's call, and I knew that we would both soon be shivering in the deep winter cold. Holmes took two more slow draughts on his cigarette, his head still dropped and his gazed fixed on the ground. Then he raised his head and looked up into the sky and at the light flakes of snow that were falling on us. I could see his entire countenance change, as I had seen it so many times in the past. His lips narrowed, and his face hardened. His eyes took on that intense burning sheen that accompanied the fixing of his mind. I knew that the game was on.

"Watson," he said without looking at me. "Please send a note off to your wife and tell her that you will not be home for dinner this evening. You will be staying over with me. I will require your assistance first thing in the morning and for the next several days. Thank you. Now, we must have a word with Mrs. Hudson."

I hastened to scribble a note and, putting my cold fingers inside my mouth, gave a sharp whistle. No one appeared. I whistled again, and I heard the door of a go-down open and close, and one of Holmes's faithful Irregulars appeared. I felt terrible looking at him. His overcoat was threadbare, and he had only thin socks and shoes on his feet. The poor child would catch his death of cold.

"Son," I said, "here is a shilling if you can deliver this note to the address on it. And there will be another shilling waiting for you in our rooms when you return, but only if you run all the way there and back. You will stay warm if you keep running. Can you do that?"

"Yes, Doctor."

He grinned and took the note I had written for my wife and began running off in the direction of Paddington. As soon as he was out of sight, I entered 221B and climbed the stairs into our front room. Holmes was sitting there, puffing on his pipe. He gestured me to be seated.

"I have asked," he said, "Mrs. Hudson to join us."

"Mrs. Hudson?"

"Yes, our landlady."

"Holmes, I know who Mrs. Hudson is. But what could she possibly have to do with the murders of two Scotland Yard inspectors?"

He declined to answer and took another long draft on his pipe. Mrs. Hudson entered the room before I could repeat my question and demand an answer. Holmes gestured for her to be seated as well.

"What is it, Mr. Holmes?" she asked.

"You are aware," he replied, "of the dreadful murders that have taken place across the street?"

"Well, I have just heard about the second one a few minutes ago. It is horrible. Just horrible. It is terribly upsetting, it is. If something like that had happened in Whitechapel, I should not be surprised. But here, on Baker Street. Why, it is just horrible."

"Yes, Mrs. Hudson, it is," said Holmes. "You have no doubt observed that I have been asked by Scotland Yard to assist in the investigation?"

"Well, I had noticed the short chap, Inspector Lestrade, coming and chatting with you and I am not at all surprised that he needs your help."

"Nor am I," said Holmes. "However, we also need your help."

"Mine?"

"Yes, Mrs. Hudson, yours. It is imperative that three days from today, first thing in the morning, that you leave and go somewhere for several days. You have a cousin, I believe, in Southampton. The weather is bound to be a few degrees warmer there. I am quite sure that you will enjoy the break and I will look after all your expenses."

The poor woman looked utterly devastated. I expected tears to form in her eyes any second.

"Mr. Holmes," she said in a trembling voice, "what have I done wrong? I have tried. Honestly, I have, never to interfere in your work. Never. I can see that you have been frightfully angry these past few days. Was it something I did? I swear, I have always kept in confidence anything I heard going on. I have never gossiped with the neighbors, not once in over twenty years, about who I saw coming and going. What have I done wrong? Why are you sending me away?"

"Oh no. No, not at all," Holmes quickly replied. "I am not sending you away. I need you to be absent for strategic reasons that will help me investigate. And I also need for you to ask Mrs. Turner across the street to look after meals for Dr. Watson and me whilst you are away."

Now the dear woman looked awfully confused.

"Has there been something wrong with the meals I have prepared, Mr. Holmes? I have tried to make them to your liking. Do you wish me to change the dishes I prepare? I do not believe, Mr. Holmes, that Mrs. Turner, would make anything better for you. But if you insist, I will ask her to come over and prepare your meals, but you might have to wait for them a while as she has five boarders of her own to look after first."

"No, no, no," said Holmes. "I do not want you to ask her to come over and serve meals here. I need for you to ask her to add Dr. Watson and me to her table and have us eat our meals there for the next two days. That is all."

For several moments, Mrs. Hudson looked at Holmes and said nothing. Then, slowly, a faint smile crept across her face.

"If that is your wish, Mr. Holmes. I shall arrange for your meals to be taken across the street And, if I might say, it is about time you took a good look at that lot of boarders. Mrs. Turner has been telling me for several weeks that there is something rotten in the state of Denmark over there. Yes, it is about time. And having me go away is a very clever excuse for you to look into the lot of them. Quite the rum lot they are, if you ask me. So, yes, Mr. Holmes, I will make those arrangements as you request, but there is one condition."

"A condition, Mrs. Hudson?"

"Yes. I have watched you work now for over twenty years, Mr. Sherlock Holmes, and I can tell when you are about to make your move. It is written all over your face. And I will have you know that there is no way on God's good earth that I want to be miles away from London when all hades is breaking loose on Baker Street. I do not mind going away, Mr. Holmes. But I am not about to leave London."

Holmes smiled warmly at her. "An excellent condition to set, Mrs. Hudson. Would you agree to be a guest at a select hotel for two nights instead?"

"That will do just fine, Mr. Holmes."

After the good woman had departed, I turned to Holmes.

"And kindly tell me just what it is you are planning for the next two days?"

"My plan, my dear Watson, is that you could, should you so choose, return to your medical practice. Alternatively, you could join me in closely observing, indeed dogging the very footsteps of the boarders of 220 Baker Street, one of whom, I suspect, might be a wickedly clever murderer. What would be your preference, my friend?"

"You are asking me if I would prefer to poke and prod the bodies of the English citizenry or join you in the pursuit of the villain who has murdered two fine police inspectors and set the rabid Press on me?"

Holmes smiled back at me. "I will take that as a 'yes' and will assume that you will join me. Together we shall breathe down the necks of this odd lot without their knowing that we are anywhere within a mile of them."

"We will be in disguise, I assume."

"Precisely. I imagine that I will become an aged, stooped seller of used books. Do you think that would be appropriate?"

I glared at Holmes before answering. "You know, I still have not forgiven you for using that on me."

"Ah, but only because it fooled you so completely. Therefore, I am sure you would recommend its use on others. And you, my dear doctor, would you mind if I were to dress you up as a common laborer?"

"As long as you dress me warmly. It is winter, you know."

Chapter Five
Following Our Suspects

At sunrise the following morning, Holmes and I were huddled on the street corner immediately south of 221B. He had procured for me, from whence I do not know, a battered but perfectly serviceable British Army greatcoat, similar to the one I wore years ago in the mountains of Afghanistan, and a warm woolen cap. I was quite comfortable. He was clad in a shabby trench coat, and I feared for his well-being, but he assured me that he had several layers of loose-fitting garments underneath. His head was kept warm by the ridiculous wig that I have described in numerous of my accounts of his previous adventures.

We had not been sitting there long before the door of Mrs. Turner's house opened, and a man emerged and began walking in the direction of Marylebone. He was a tall chap and was walking quickly. His hat was pulled down, and his collar turned up to keep out the cold, and it was difficult to see his face. At the corner, he turned west on Marylebone and started off towards Paddington, but shortly after crossing Edgeware Road, he left the main thoroughfare and turned right on to one of the side streets. After another two turns, I grabbed Holmes by the forearm.

"This is the street that I live on," I whispered.

"I am certain," he said, "that it is not a coincidence."

The fellow appeared to be looking at the numbers on the houses and to my horror, he stopped directly in front of my home. He stood and gazed at it for several minutes. Whilst he was doing so, it was possible to get a good look at his face. He had a somewhat dark complexion and jet-black hair.

Holmes had his spyglass out and was watching the man intently.

"He is the Indian fellow, all right. Quite tall and athletic. However, he is not particularly dark in color. Many shades lighter than the Tamils. I suspect that Mrs. Turner was correct in deducing that he is Anglo-Indian."

"But what is he doing looking at my home? My wife is there now and except for the maid, all alone."

"He will not do anything hostile this morning," said Holmes. "He is obviously on his way to some place for some purpose, and whatever it is, it is important to him. I suspect that he realized that he has time to spare before his appointment and finding himself very near to your residence, he decided to take a look. Ah, but now he moves on. Come."

I was utterly unnerved by what I had just observed, but Holmes seemed to take it as of no account, so I followed along as we rounded the corner and came to the front entrance of St. Mary's Hospital on the north side of Paddington. A family of Gypsies was seated on the ground by the gate, begging. To my surprise, the Indian stopped, squatted down and chatted with them for several minutes before taking out some coins and giving them to the father. The look on the Gypsy's face indicated that it was a generous almsgiving. The doctor then stood and uncertainly checked his watch before entering the hospital.

"What is he doing?" I wondered out loud.

"Most likely applying for a position at the hospital," said Holmes. "And most likely, he will not be successful."

"Why do you say that?"

"This fine hospital is administered by a very competent order of Catholic sisters who graciously provide care to people of all faiths, colors, and creeds. However, they are also shrewd businesswomen who know that their patients demand to be treated by an English Catholic doctor and have an aversion to removing their clothing in front of a man they would consider a snake-charmer, regardless of his medical pedigree."

"Holmes, you horrify me. That is a terrible thing to say about common English people."

"I horrify myself, but please observe. Our man will reappear in short order and will not be happy."

He was right. We sat amongst the waiting patients for no more than twenty minutes before seeing the Indian doctor emerge, his face clouded and his head down. He walked quickly out of the building, pushing the door open with a hard jab. Upon reaching the pavement, he turned and looked back at the hospital and then spat on the ground before walking to the cab stand.

We clambered into the cab immediately behind his and Holmes told the driver to follow the one that had just departed. Soon we were rattling through the morning traffic, traveling east along Marylebone. The cab we were following passed Baker Street, and then the Marylebone High Street before turning south on Harley Street. If the fellow was looking for a medical practice in which to seek employment, he had certainly come to the right neighborhood.

His cab stopped in front of one of the quite well-to-do surgeries. I knew the place. It was the medical practice of Dr. Richard St. John Long, the distinguished physician, and pillar of the BMA who treated many of the wealthiest men and women of London. He had kindly attended the reception that was held for me at the Langham and had passed along encouraging words, although I suspected they were more intended to keep me writing stories than healing the sick.

Holmes and I sat in our cab watching and waiting. Holmes had his spyglass at the ready, but it was almost an hour before the young doctor emerged. The difference in his posture and gait from what we saw at St. Mary's could not have been more obvious.

"The fellow," said Holmes, "appears to be smiling. There is a decided bounce in his steps. Either he has just been cured of some terrible disease, or he has secured a position."

"I would be surprised," I said, "if it were either."

"As you know this medical chap, St. John Long, would you mind dropping in and having a chat with him and seeing if there is anything that can be gleaned about his recent visitor?"

All doctors are bound by strict confidentiality when discussing the affairs and symptoms of their patients, unless, of course, they are speaking to other doctors in which case they are irrepressible gossips. I assured Holmes that I would do my best. I doffed my coat and hat in the cab and entered the tastefully furnished office. I could not help noticing a collection of Strand magazines strewn across the coffee and end tables of his waiting room, some dating back a decade or more.

"Why, John Watson," came the ebullient greeting as I poked my head inside his office. "What a surprise. Do come in. To what do I owe this honor?"

We chatted briefly about the recent reception, and I answered his many questions about Sherlock Holmes. Then I casually posed a question about the Indian fellow I had seen exiting the office as I was approaching.

"Oh, that fellow. Yes, quite a well-qualified young man. Exactly who I need on my staff."

"Indeed? I would not have thought that an Indian fellow would have many prospects in this neighborhood," I said.

"Oh, quite the opposite," he said. "Over the past few years, we have had no end of very well-off Hindus, Mohammedans, and Sikhs, and who knows who else depart the Raj and move to London. And they all need doctors and are much more at ease, especially the women folk, with one of their own than a white man. We may be their colonial masters, but when they are paying the piper, they call the tune. It is just the way they are. I have been looking for a fellow like that Dr. Roulston for some time now. Being from Calcutta, he is quite the expert on all those nasty, awful ailments that those poor folks acquire from insects, bad water, snake bites, damp air and the like, about which I know so very little. He is almost a perfect addition to my staff."

"Almost, you say? What does he lack?"

"A wife."

"Oh, come, come."

"No, I am in earnest. All those Indian women are much happier if they have an Indian doctor and they know he has a wife."

"But why?"

"Because, if they do not like how he treats them, they will go and complain to his wife and then she will make life miserable for her husband until he behaves. It is just the way they are, my good man."

We chatted a bit longer and then I excused myself and reported back to Holmes. He made no comment on my observations and merely nodded sagaciously. When I had finished, he smiled.

"Excellent, Watson. I have a contact in Calcutta to whom I shall send off a wire asking for confirmation on the story given by the young doctor. Now, however, as we have lost our Indian, I suggest that we return to Baker Street and see if another one of Mrs. Turner's boarders goes anywhere this afternoon."

We did so, and upon arriving there, I rushed into the sandwich shop that had recently opened beneath 221B. Whilst Holmes and I were unceremoniously eating a quick lunch by the bay window, another one of Mrs. Turner's boarders emerged, a woman this time. We hurriedly bounced down our stairs and followed her. She walked to the Underground station and boarded the recently opened Bakerloo line. We did the same and followed her for three stops to Piccadilly Circus. Once there, she exited the station and, walking quite proudly, entered the Criterion Bar and Restaurant, the very same establishment in which I had encountered young Stamford so many years ago. The place had moved decidedly up the ladder of taste and cost from the days it catered to the needs and wants of impoverished returning soldiers from Afghanistan.

"We can join her," said Holmes as he handed the fare to our driver and dismissed him.

"We are not exactly dressed, "I said, "like the customers they are now accustomed to serving. I dare say, we might get the bum's rush."

"I think not," said Holmes and we sauntered in and found a table that allowed us a clear view of the woman we had followed in. One of the waiters immediately approached our table and was, I am certain, about to suggest that we seek some other bar in which to relax ourselves. Holmes, with a flourish, laid five sovereigns on the table and the waiter's demeanor changed abruptly.

"Ah, yes, gentlemen. And how might I be of service to you?"

We were soon sipping two generous snifters of excellent brandy whilst surreptitiously regarding the lady.

"Very well, Watson," said Holmes. "Tell me what you observe and what you might deduce from your observations."

Holmes loved playing this game with me as I still, even after so many years, failed to either see or reason when looking at someone intently. However, I played along.

"She must be the Welsh woman," I said. "She certainly has that look about her. No longer young. About our age, but still quite handsome. No longer thin either. Ample around both bosom and buttocks. Well-dressed, I must say. Her clothes are made from expensive fine fabrics. The hat is excessively large but quite stylish. She ordered a decent glass of claret. That, and her attire say that she is not lacking in money. I do not see a ring on her finger, but I suspect that she has been married in the past. Her face is pleasant, perhaps bordering on florid; more than is caused by the cold weather. She seems quite the jovial type, very confident. What else should I have noticed, Holmes?"

"Not bad, Watson. Not bad at all. You might have added that when she entered the *maître d'* greeted her by name. When she approached her table, the barman gave a warm smile. She has exchanged familiar glances with three of the gentleman who are sitting at the bar or other tables. The Criterion caters now to the upper classes and the chaps who are its customers, with the exception of you and me, are a well-heeled lot. She appears to know the clientele rather well and is exceptionally comfortable in the company of men. Now, did you happen to get a close look at her smile?"

"Not particularly. It seemed pleasant and attractive enough."

"Indeed, it was. However, between her two front teeth, there is a distinct gap. Does that remind you of a character from your lessons as a schoolboy?"

I searched the recess of my memory and replied. "The Wife of Bath?"

"Precisely. And what were you told that such a dental feature signified?"

"For Chaucer," I said, "it was a mark of sensuality; a tendency to indulge in the pleasures of the flesh. But come now, Holmes, that is mere folklore and superstition."

"Quite so, but such longstanding beliefs invariably find their origins in the shared experience of the people who believe them. I suspect that in the case of our lady from Wales, there may be some truth."

I harrumphed. "I fear you impugn the woman's character. All we know is that she is friendly towards gentlemen and nothing more."

"Perhaps. Let us relax and keep our eyes on her."

Within another five minutes, one of the finely attired chaps who had been sitting at the bar, rose and came over to the table where Mrs. Owen was seated. After a brief exchange of conversation that engendered smiles from both parties, he seated himself at the same table and ordered another round of drinks.

"Isn't that Lord Downash of Horton-sub-Namdon?" I asked.

"The same. He has a reputation for being overly fond of the ladies, but that is to be expected of a liberal."

Mrs. Owen and his lordship chatted amiably for another ten minutes, interrupted by outbursts of joyful laughter. They quite clearly enjoyed each other's company. I then saw him lean in quite close to here and whisper in her ear. Then he paid the bill, and the two of them rose and began to walk towards the door.

"We shall follow them discreetly," said Holmes and the two of us shuffled our way out of the Criterion and back on to the pavement in front of Piccadilly Circus. The lord and Mrs. Owen had crossed west over Lower Regent Street and entered the posh new Piccadilly Hotel.

"Dear me," I said, "is she a courtesan? Is he about to engage in an unlawful dalliance with her?"

"Quite possibly," said Holmes. "I shall have to observe. Perhaps you should wait here on the pavement in case either one of them makes a hurried exit."

"Holmes, you cannot just walk into a select hotel looking as you do."

"I am delivering a book to the good lady."

He stumbled toward the door of the hotel, and I waited. Five minutes later he reappeared.

"Quite the interesting woman," he said.

"Explain, please."

"When she, not his lordship, approached the front desk, the reception clerk immediately handed the room key to her without asking her name or room number. Then the two of them walked over to the staircase. I approached the desk and noted the empty pigeonhole from which the key had been extracted. Room 341. If my memory serves me correctly, it is a corner suite of rooms and as fine an accommodation as is offered in London. It would seem that she is a longstanding guest. I told the clerk that I was delivering some books that Mrs. Owen had purchased and would he mind if I took them up to her room. His reply was mildly surprising."

"Yes?"

"He said 'Who?'"

"I repeated her name and added that I had just seen her walk into the hotel with her husband. He gave me a very puzzled look and then replied, 'Oh, yes, of course, Mrs. Owen. Yes, she just came in, but she asked that she not be disturbed.

and as she is one of our long-term guests, I must respect her requests. If you wish, you may leave the books here, and I will look after that matter for you.'

"I thanked him, claimed that the books had to be signed for personally, and promised to return later when the dear lady was not occupied. We chatted for a few minutes. It turns out that he is quite the bibliophile and delighted to find another one. A friendship with the chap will prove useful in the future."

"Well," I said, "books or no, the Welsh woman most certainly does seem to have some very unusual moral standards."

"Perhaps," said Holmes. "Perhaps she is merely a very astute woman, or perhaps utterly ruthless. I will need to make further inquiries."

That ended my surveillance adventures for the day, and I retired to a supper at 221B. Holmes ate little and spoke less. On several occasions, I noticed him gripping his knife and fork tightly and his eyes blazing in anger. I was most certain that he would not rest until he had struck down those who murdered police officers that he respected and sought to humiliate him by doing so.

Chapter Six
Bless Me, Father

The next morning found Holmes and me again on the street and in disguise. At shortly after eight o'clock the door of Mrs. Turner's boarding house opened, and the Indian doctor fellow emerged.

"We shall ignore him," said Holmes. "I hope to hear back from Calcutta by the end of the day."

We waited another half an hour before the German woman stepped out onto the pavement.

"Excellent timing," said Holmes. "Let us see what our fräulein does with her time whilst in London."

Like the Welsh woman, the German also strode toward the Underground station, howbeit in a much more stately manner than the older woman the day before. We followed her on to the Bakerloo Line and exited behind her at Charring Cross. From there she rounded the south end of Trafalgar Square and crossed through the Admiralty Arch. She then turned right and walked through a narrow alley between buildings and emerged on to Carlton House Terrace.

"She is walking toward Prussia House," said Holmes, "The German Legation."

At the gate of the building, she stopped and handed a note to the guard. Then she turned and walked back along Carlton Terrace until she came to a small café whose signboard advertised that it specialized in German food. She sat at a table near the door, ordered a coffee and waited. Holmes and I had found a bench across the street and, like two undesirables, sat and watched her. The contrast to the Welsh woman could not have been more telling. She did not even look at the waiter who brought her a demitasse, and her posture radiated haughtiness to all around. After some ten minutes, she turned her head and looked down the street, continuing to look for several more minutes. Then she rose quickly to her feet and stepped away from her table. The object of her intentions was a young man walking toward her. He was tall, blond, and dressed in a military style of overcoat. We could see her face break into a smile as he approached and the two of them threw their arms around each other and held the embrace for a rather long period of time. Then they sat down and began to chat. At first, both were clearly enjoying each other's company and then their faces clouded over, and they drew their heads together.

"A singularly revealing encounter," mused Holmes as he continued to regard the couple through his spyglass.

"In what way?" I asked.

"The two are known to each other, have not seen each other for some time, and share a strong, affectionate attraction."

"Wife and husband?" I said. "Lovers?"

"Goodness no, Watson. Come now, what did you notice about their embrace? Was it the type of embrace you would expect to receive from your loving wife if you had not seen her for some time?"

I hesitated and reflected on that one. "No. I suppose not. It was quite loving and warm and enthusiastic, but no more than their shoulders touched each other. It was completely devoid of any sensual contact."

"Precisely. Now, use the glass and look at both of the faces. What do you observe?"

I looked, and then smiled, and handed the glass back. "A distinct family resemblance," I said. "They are brother and sister."

"Exactly. And although they are thrilled to see each other, they are also involved together in some sort of secret and possibly nefarious activities. As the brother appears to have emerged from the German Legation building, we can consider the possibility that some subterfuge and intrigue may be in play. I will have to make further inquiries concerning her."

"Her name," I said, "is Schmidt. It is the most common name in Germany. How will you trace her?"

"I would wager, Watson, if you were willing, that her name is not Schmidt and that Schmidt is only her alias. She has assumed it to protect her true identity. But I will also wager that her brother, who is apparently an officer in the German Legation, is listed under his true family name, as the Germans are highly regimented in such matters. We merely learn his name, and we shall have hers."

I did not accept his wager. We sat and continued to observe the couple as they whispered to each other. At one point in the conversation, the young man took out a notebook and began to scribble somewhat furiously. I could not imagine what they were up to.

After a full half hour of observing them, Holmes rose from the bench. "Come. There is no more to be seen here. Let us return to Baker Street and see if we can track any more of the motley crew."

Holmes insisted that we wait yet again in the winter cold so that we could follow another boarder if he were to emerge from Mrs. Turner's. I objected and argued that we could sit comfortably by the bay window in 221B, with our overcoats at the ready, and be on the tail of our quarry with only a few seconds sacrificed. He grudgingly agreed, but I suspected that he was not altogether dissatisfied with his acquiescence.

For a full two hours, we sat in silence and watched the door across the street. At just after the noon hour, it opened, and a small, thin man emerged.

"That is the one Mrs. Turner called Tarker," said Holmes. "Come, let us see what he is up to."

Yet again we followed our man into the Baker Street Station but this time boarded a train on the older Metropolitan Line. Our journey was much longer, taking us all the way to Aldgate, the final station on the line, before getting off. The cars were crowded when we started the journey, but by the time we passed Euston, many of the passengers had departed, leaving sufficient seats for everyone. Some read books or the newspaper, some chatted with their neighbor, and some rested their heads on the back of the seats and dozed off. Mr. Tarker remained standing. He constantly shifted his position, and his eyes never ceased furtively darting around the rail car. Several times I felt his gaze rest on Holmes and me.

"That fellow," I whispered to Holmes, "is as skittish as a cat in a dog kennel."

"Yes," said Holmes. "We may face some challenges in following him. He has seen us and will not forget us."

At Aldgate, we departed the Underground and climbed the stairs back to the pavement and the open air. I was not familiar with the section of London in which we had found ourselves. It marked the beginning of the Whitechapel borough of London's East End and had a reputation for all sorts of unpleasant goings-on. Fortunately, we did not have to walk any distance along the streets, as our man made his way straight to an old pub, The Hoop and Grapes. I recalled reading that this establishment had survived the Great Fire of 1666 and prided itself on not having a single window, door frame or step that was still square. It had been noted several times in the Press as the place where the police had apprehended some petty and several not-so-petty criminals

"We cannot follow him there looking as we do," said Holmes, grabbing my forearm and halting our walk. "He will know immediately that we are following him. Please wait here and hold my coat until I return."

He quickly pulled off his overcoat and handed it to me and just as quickly removed his beard and wig. Then he pulled a woolen cap from his pockets and placed it on his head. Finally, he produced a large ornate cross that he hung around his neck.

"Do I look priestly enough?" he asked.

"Remarkably so," I said. "But should a priest be walking into a pub that has a reputation for harboring criminals and prostitutes?"

"Where else does one go if one is looking for lost souls in need of saving?"

I waited a full half hour for Holmes to return, making use of my time by recording the details of the last two days in my notebook. Just as I put my pencil back in my pocket, Father Sherlock came out of the pub.

"Bless me, Father," I said. "Pray impart your teachings to me this afternoon."

For the first time since this case began, Holmes offered back a faint smile.

"Mr. Tarker in consorting with known criminals. Upon entering, he sat at the bar and spoke to the barkeep, who immediately went into one of the back rooms. He returned, followed by a fellow I recognized. You might recall his name, Roger Sneyd-Kynnersley."

I did recall the name. He was a schoolmaster and a scoundrel who had been charged with using his school boys to commit countless robberies. But the evidence against him was thin, as his charges refused to testify or, if they did, lied through their young teeth. He was convicted only with possessing stolen goods and given a light sentence.

"What could he and Tarker have to do with each other."

"The exact nature of their engagement, I do not know. However, when Tarker emerged from the back office he immediately approached the bar and ordered a very select whiskey, which he paid for with a five-pound note. He would appear to have been contracted by Sneyd-Kynnersley to carry out some task, and I would be quite certain that whatever he has done or is about to do is criminal in nature."

"Should you alert Scotland Yard?"

Holmes pondered his answer. "Perhaps I should but doing so could alert Tarker and the others that someone is spying on them and they would be fools if they could not deduce that it was me. So, we shall wait until we have sprung our trap on them before diverting any involvement by the Yard."

We waited for another half hour before concluding that our man was intent on spending his remuneration in the pub and it would be a waste of our time to sit in the cold until he staggered out. So, we returned to the Aldgate Station and took a train back to Baker Street.

By tea time we were back sitting by the bay window as the late afternoon light faded from the sky. We enjoyed a cup of cocoa that Mrs. Hudson had kindly prepared to take the chill out of our bones. We had just requested that she begin to prepare dinner when Holmes suddenly stood up brought his face to the window.

"Mrs. Hudson," he shouted. "put a hold on dinner until we return! Come, Watson. The fifth boarder has just left Number 220. Quick, we can catch him."

We grabbed out coats and scampered down the stairs. Holmes opened the door to Baker Street and then stepped back inside immediately, pulling the door closed behind him.

"He is not going anywhere. He is standing on the pavement likely waiting for a cab to appear."

He opened the door just a crack and peered out into the twilight.

"There is a cab coming. Yes. He has hailed it. Ah, we are in luck, Watson. There is another one close behind. Come now, quickly. We shall have to grab it before it passes."

Holmes ran out into the road and raised his hand in front of the cab. The driver pulled hard on the reins, causing the poor horse to rear up. In no uncertain terms and several quite certain oaths, the driver let Holmes know of his displeasure.

Holmes apologized and offered the fellow a sovereign. The string of oaths ceased, and we quickly began our pursuit of the other cab. We followed it south on Baker Street, across Oxford and then to Hyde Park Corner. There, the cab we were following stopped. Mr. Clarke got out, immediately hailed another cab and continued into Mayfair. It came to a stop on one of the most exclusive streets in London, a well-lit mews just beyond Grosvenor Square. We pulled in behind it, about half a block back, and Holmes took out his spyglass. The winter sun had set, but there was sufficient light from the street lamps for us to watch as the boarder who Mrs. Turner had identified as John Clarke climbed out of the cab in front of us. He was splendidly dressed in a tailored frock coat and a bowler hat and carried a large valise. He paid the driver and turned and walked up to the door of the nearest row house.

"Whatever is he doing in this neighborhood?" I wondered out loud.

"And why would he be carrying an empty piece of luggage," added Holmes, "to a house that appears to be uninhabited?"

The front of the house had numerous windows, but there was no sign of light coming from any of them. The front door area was easily seen in the light from the street lamp, and I watched as the fellow put down his valise and knocked several times on the brass door knocker. The door did not immediately open, and he waited about half a minute before knocking again.

"Good heavens," said Holmes as he fixed his gaze through his spyglass. "He is knocking with one hand and appears to be picking the lock with the other, without even looking at what he is doing."

A moment later, the door opened, and the fellow entered the house, closing the door behind him.

Holmes lowered his glass. "Watson, did you see that? I have never in all my dealings with criminals watched anyone so brazenly walk up to a door in full view, expertly pick a lock with one hand in less than a minute and walk inside. That was singularly impressive. I do not know who this fellow is, but he is an utterly brilliant thief. Come, let us try to observe through the back windows of the house."

We got out of our cab and ran along the alley behind the row of houses. On reaching the lot of the house that had just been entered, we climbed over a small back garden wall and silently worked our way to the kitchen window. The house was in darkness, but we could see the faint flickering of a light from an electric torch somewhere in the front rooms. The light danced around for some ten minutes before it became much stronger as the fellow holding it walked out into the central hallway. From the movement and dimming of the light, I could see that he was working his way up the stairs. Holmes and I moved back from the kitchen window and could observe a faint glow now coming from the windows on the second floor.

"What is he doing?" I asked.

"It looks as if he is robbing the place," said Holmes. "And I do not believe that in my many years of observing criminal behavior, I have ever witnessed anyone so utterly fearless. I expect that in a few more minutes, he will leave the house with his valise packed full of plate and jewelry. Come, back to the front of the house."

We had not been back on the street long before the door of the house opened, the thief emerged, and he closed the door behind him. Then he turned and faced the door, lowering his right hand to the lock.

"He is locking the door behind him," said Holmes. "The man is inhumanly skilled."

He then left the porch, descended the steps and, now carrying an obviously heavier valise, walked toward the corner.

"Are you not going to apprehend him?" I asked. "I have my service revolver with me. We should be able to hold him until a policeman shows up."

"No," said Holmes. "If he is the murderer of the inspectors, I do not want to have him charged and tried for mere house theft before we find the evidence we need to send him to the gallows."

From the shadows, we watched the man hail a cab and head back towards Hyde Park.

"Enough," said Holmes. "It is time now for us to lay our trap. Your breakfast tomorrow morning, Watson, will be served at 220 Baker street."

Chapter Seven
Preparing to be Murdered

Before the sun had risen the following morning, Holmes and I were sitting at the table waiting for the return of Mrs. Hudson. At a quarter past seven, we heard the door open, and she ascended the stairs.

"Your breakfast across the street has been arranged, gentlemen. All you have to do is arrive there in fifteen minutes, and Mrs. Turner will show you to the table. She was already busy preparing the food when I told her that I had been called away on an urgent family matter, so she will not have time to let her boarders know they will have company before they appear for breakfast. Now, if you will excuse me, I will be off. If you need me, you may send a note to the

Langham. Good day, Mr. Holmes, Dr. Watson. Mind you; I expect to hear every last detail of what you will be up to. I do not expect to have to read about it in the newspapers first."

She smiled, picked up her overnight bag and departed.

"Do we," I asked Holmes, "have a plan for this escapade?"

"No. We shall merely chat with them amicably. They will not be expecting us, so nothing untoward is likely to happen. Kindly follow my lead. We shall return at dinner. By then, whoever has been responsible for the murders, if indeed it is one of them and I suspect it is, will be prepared for us."

"Prepared to do what?"

"To murder us, of course. Come now, we would not want breakfast to get cold."

We crossed over Baker Street and knocked on the door of Number 220. Mrs. Turner opened it, looking rather rushed and put upon, but she smiled all the same.

"Please, gentlemen, come it. I had to water down the porridge a little, but the rest of the food will have decent portions. Please, come in to the dining room."

We followed her into the dining room of the house, where five boarders were already seated. They looked up at us, and I struggled to refrain from laughing at the looks on their faces.

"Good morning, all," said Mrs. Turner. "We have two extra for breakfast. Mrs. Hudson across the way had to run off on an urgent family matter, so her boarders are joining us. She does the same for me when I have to be away. All of you likely know these two, as they are somewhat famous. Please say good morning to Mr. Sherlock Holmes and Dr. Watson."

The three men stumbled and tottered as they pushed their chairs back and stood up. As the room was already cramped, Holmes smiled and graciously introduced us.

"Please, gentlemen," he said, "no need to get up. So sorry to have intruded on your mealtime. Please be seated. And ladies, good morning."

We quickly took our seats, and before any of the slackened jaws had closed, Holmes carried on as if such a breakfast event were as common as dirt.

"My colleague and I," he began, "have already been introduced by the good Mrs. Turner. Perhaps each of you could introduce yourselves to us so that we may do you the courtesy of remembering your names. You, sir. Who might you be?"

He looked directly at the large Indian fellow who was, I had to agree, quite the powerful looking chap, for an Indian that is. The man looked more than a little nonplussed for a moment before recovering.

"Who, sir? Me, sir? Ah, very, very good, sir. Yes, Mr. Holmes, sir, I am Govinda Roulston. Dr. Govinda Roulston."

"Delighted to meet you, doctor," said Holmes. "And at which hospital do you practice?"

"Umm ... none yet, Mr. Holmes. None yet. I have only recently arrived in London from Calcutta and am applying for a position at several hospitals. I expect that I will be accepted soon."

"Excellent. We wish you great success. And you, madam," he said addressing the Welsh lady. "What brings you to this corner of our great city. I suspect that you are not a native Londoner. What is your name and where might you be from?"

"I am from Caerdydd, sir. My enw, my name I should say, is Alwyn Owen. *Mrs.* Alwyn Owen."

"And now from London. Well done. And what was it that brought you to the great metropolis?"

"My meistr died. I was left a bit of arian, so I moved to Llundain, sir."

"I cannot blame you, madam. I would have done the same."

"And you, sir? By what name are you known?"

He was looking at a man of average height and weight who was exceptionally well-dressed. His head was bald, and he sported a beard and a pince-nez, which he adjusted with his fine, manicured, pale hand. He was unmistakably the thief we had observed the night before.

"You may address me, Mr. Holmes, as Sir John Clarke."

"A pleasure to do so, Sir John. Is the 'Clarke' with an 'e' or without."

"With. And is it Holmes with an 'l' or without?"

"With, sir. We both bear the burden of unnecessary letters in our names."

I laughed, and a couple of the boarders joined me. Sir John did not.

To the striking, tall blonde woman, Holmes now smiled.

"And you, miss. Your bearing and countenance suggest that you are also a visitor to London. From Germany, perhaps?"

"Ja. I am from Deutschland."

"And your business in England, Fräulein?"

"What business is that of yours?"

"None at all, except that in my line of work I have met countless people and might be able to refer you to those who could assist in your endeavors."

The woman gave a haughty shrug. "*Ich bezweifle das*. But if you must know, research into military history, I am doing."

"And do you need any introductions at Sandhurst, perhaps?"

"Nein."

"Very well, then. You, my good man. Who might you be?" He spoke to the small, wiry fellow on the far side of the table. The man did not look up but continued to look and speak to the English breakfast that had recently been deposited in front of him.

"Name's Tarker."

"A pleasure to meet you, Mr. Tarker. And what is your line of work, sir?"

"A laborer."

"Ah, a man who works with his hands and earns an honest day's wages."

The fellow made no response. He looked up for a moment and nodded and then picked up his knife and fork and gave his full attention to his meal.

Holmes made a few more pleasant comments, and the entire group of us stopped speaking and began to devour our breakfast until Sir John put down his fork and glared at Holmes.

"The chap beside you is a doctor," he said. "You did not tell us what it is that you do, Mr. Holmes."

"Oh, dear. How thoughtless of me. I am a detective."

"I am not familiar with that profession," said Sir John. "Do they teach that at Oxford or Cambridge?"

"No, sir. I am afraid that my reasoning mind was formed in the school of facts. I stick to the facts, sir." said Holmes.

"Hmm. Pity," was the reply.

"Indeed, it is," agreed Holmes. "Ah, Fräulein, would you mind passing the pitcher of water? Water and fresh fruit-juice are all I drink these days. My studies, such as they were, informed me that alcohol and caffeine such as are found in tea and coffee are poisonous to the body, and I have sworn off all such substances, unless, of course, someone is proposing a toast, in which case I might imbibe."

That was news to me, and if it were true, such a decision must have been taken sometime following last evening's late dinner, which Holmes had washed down with several glasses of claret.

Within a few minutes, the Tarker chap had wolfed down his meal and rose from his chair and departed without a word. By five minutes after that, the other four members lay down their cutlery and rose and, after a few polite words, departed. Holmes and I were left alone finishing our breakfast.

"Really, Holmes," I said. "Since when ..."

"Shush! ... ask me later. Now please, Watson. Enjoy this fine meal that Mrs. Turner has prepared. It will fortify you for your medical services throughout the day. And then please meet me back at 221B at six this evening, so that we may return to this friendly establishment for our evening meal."

He rose and left me alone. However, it was a fine English breakfast, and I was determined not to let it go to waste, so I relaxed and enjoyed it, alone.

Six o'clock found me back at Baker Street and prepared to cross over to 220 for supper. Holmes was stretched out on the sofa, clad in his dressing gown, smoking a cigarette and reading a journal.

"You asked me here for six," I said.

"Ah, yes. My apologies. But I received a note to say that dinner had been postponed until nine."

"Nine? Why?"

"Apparently two of our neighbors had obligations in the City. That was what it said in the note."

"What do any of them do in the City?"

"Nothing."

"Holmes, please."

"I am certain it was merely a ruse to postpone our time together this evening."

"But why?"

"So they could murder us at a more appropriate hour."

"Oh, is that so? Well then, if I am going to be murdered, Holmes, then the least you could do is explain how and when it is going to happen and by whom."

Holmes put down his journal and smiled at me.

"I do wish I knew and that is what we are about to find out."

"Holmes."

"Really, Watson. It has become rather obvious, has it not? Two healthy police inspectors made visits to Mrs. Turner's. They then appear dead next door, having died, as you have borne witness, somewhere between morning and mid-day. Yet not one them entered Camden House anywhere near those times. Therefore, they must have been drugged earlier, quite heavily sedated in fact. They were then taken at night to the empty room next door whilst unconscious and then killed by means unknown a few hours later. I do not know how they were drugged, or who did that and moved their bodies, or how they were killed. Therefore, we shall present ourselves to the killer as the next victims and find out. There is no doubt that I am one of the intended targets and you are likely to be as well due to your guilt by association."

"Holmes."

"Oh, come, come, Watson. They will not get away with it. Have you brought your service revolver?"

"Of course."

"Excellent. There on the chair and the coffee table are your armor and weapon of choice for this evening."

I looked and observed a heavy leather long-sleeve shirt lying across the chair, and a small pewter goblet on the table.

"Holmes, what is the meaning of these?"

"You and I shall don the leather shirts prior to going for dinner. They are not terribly comfortable, but they do protect against anyone inserting a hypodermic needle into one's torso. Do you recognize the goblets?"

I picked it up and looked at it.

"Mrs. Turner had a large set of these on her sideboard," I said.

"Yes, she still does. Except that set is now two short. Put one in your pocket."

"What in the world for? If I am to defend myself, a blackjack would be of more use."

"Oh, my dear Watson. You will not be physically assaulted. You will be drugged. At least that is what will be attempted. Either the killer stabbed his victim with a needle or, more likely, he placed a powerful mixture of laudanum in a glass of wine or whiskey and gave it to the inspectors. I have prepared them by telling them that the only liquids I now ingest are water and fruit juices, neither of which is strong enough in taste to cover the taste of laudanum. They have only one choice."

"A toast," I said. "To our dear departed Queen."

"Precisely. I would not be at all surprised if Forbes and Jones were also invited to join in such a toast when they came to visit. Or perhaps it was a toast to her dissolute son, our Prince of Wales and future king."

"But why steal the goblets?"

"I did not steal them, Watson. I merely borrowed them. You shall keep the empty one in your pocket and shall slyly substitute it for the full one that is given to you before raising it to your lips. Then, when no one is observing, you may pour the full one out on the carpet beneath the table and slip that one into your pocket. Do you think you can pull it off, Watson, even if you know they are trying to kill you?"

"I am your man."

"Capital. I knew you would be."

"Holmes, if someone is about to attempt to murder me, would you mind telling me which one of the odd lot that you suspect above the others."

"As I have told you in the past, Watson, it is always a mistake to theorize ..."

"Confound it, Holmes. I know what you have said a hundred times. Just answer my question. If someone is about to murder me, who is it likely to be?"

He took a slow, annoying puff on a cigarette.

"Anyone of them could, I suppose. But there were several peculiar things about the thief who calls himself Sir John that I found quite curious. Did you notice anything about him?"

"Other than his brilliant means of robbing a house? No. What did you notice."

"His bald head."

"That is not exactly a trait that distinguishes murderers."

"No," agreed Holmes. "But he is not naturally bald. He shaves his head. Unfortunately, he neglected to before breakfast this morning, with the result that a fine sprouting of stubble could be observed. And did you notice his eyes?"

I thought for a moment. "He was wearing a pince-nez. A fairly strong set. They distorted his eyes when I looked at him."

"Ah, an excellent observation. Watson. However, he was not wearing the pince-nez when we entered the room, and he pulled them from his pocket immediately upon seeing us.

When shaking some salt on to his breakfast, he held them up so he could see clearly. Obviously, he is using them to disguise himself. He was worried that I might recognize him."

"And did you?"

"Of course. He claims that his name is Clarke, but on the register at Mrs. Turner's, he signed without an 'e.' That is quite obviously not his true name."

"What is it?"

"Clay."

"Clay? Not John Clay? That fellow? The 'do not touch me with your filthy hands, I have royal blood in my veins' bank robber?"

"Precisely. I have only looked at him once, and that was in the dark basement of the City and Suburban Bank. After that, Inspector Jones took over the case and put him away for a rather long time. But I did get a good look at his eyes, and they have not changed, even after his years in Newgate."

"And his reason for wanting to murder you and the fellow from Scotland Yard?"

"Revenge. He prides himself on his brilliance and has been seething for years in prison knowing that I easily bested him. Plus, he could never go back to his brilliant criminal ways as long as I am alive. I would have known his telltale signs as soon as he tried."

"But he tried and succeeded last night."

"Ah, yes. But the occupants of that house are away. The theft is not likely to be discovered for another fortnight. I suspect that by that time he expects to have done away with me. You too, quite possibly."

"And you think he is now going to try to kill us both."

"No. I only have deduced that he is the most likely suspect. We shall have to wait until whoever it is makes his, or her, move before I know for sure. Can you play the role until that time?"

"I am sure I can."

"Excellent. I was sure you would be up for the game. Now, please relax yourself until it is time to dress for dinner and depart."

I was not sure what a man did to relax prior to being murdered, but a copy of the *Times* for the day was strewn on the floor, and I amused myself with it.

At a quarter to nine, I pulled the leather shirt on beneath my mine and adjusted my pockets to carry both my service revolver and the small pewter goblet. Holmes did the same, and just before leaving 221B he put a small Webley into his pocket and handed me a blackjack.

"Just in case," he smiled.

We crossed over to 220 and were met with a jubilant Mrs. Turner, who showed us into the dining room. This time the rest of the boarders rose and greeted us as if we were long lost friends. The dinner was a pleasant affair. We dined on an excellent roast of beef, complete with Yorkshire pudding. The conversation was lively and interesting, although I had the strange feeling that I was listening to speeches that had been rehearsed and practiced before being delivered. As Mrs. Turner was clearing away the dishes from the main course, the Welsh woman put her hand on the landlady's forearm.

"Mrs. Turner," she said sweetly. "We've kept you so late. Please, just leave the dishes. We'll look after them. You need to retire for the evening. Several other heads nodded and made murmurs of agreement. Mrs. Turner smiled kindly back to them and departed.

Sir John rose.

"It was just a few days ago," he began, quite sonorously, "that our beloved Queen Victoria passed on to her greater reward."

He continued for several minutes saying all sorts of things about the Old Girl. As he did so, Mr. Tarker placed small pewter goblets in front of every one's place setting. The fräulein followed him with a sherry decanter in each hand and filled the goblets.

Sir John reached the end of his oration with "A toast to the Queen."

We all reached for our goblets. I felt a kick from Holmes under the table and whilst pushing my chair back to stand, quickly slid my hand into my pocket and extracted my empty goblet whilst concealing the full one behind my back. We all raised our glasses and sat down again.

No sooner had we done so, but the German woman and Mr. Tarker came around again with more sherry. This time it was the doctor from Calcutta who rose to speak. He was nowhere near as articulate as Sir John but in his heavy Indian accent proposed a toast to our soon-to-be new king, the current Prince of Wales. He said many complimentary things about Prince Bertie which struck me as absurd as we all knew that he was a bounder of a womanizer and a thorough cad.

Whilst he was expounding, I slid my hand well under the table and silently poured my second full glass of sherry onto the carpet. I could sense Holmes doing the same thing.

We all stood when the toast was called for, and this time I raised my now empty glass to my lips and concealed again the full one. I was afraid that they might go on with toasts to all the royal princes, dead and alive, and that I would end up with a rather large puddle under my chair, but they stopped at two. Once we were seated, Holmes began one of his favorite stories about his time in Tibet, posing as Sigerson, and his conversation with the Head Lama.

I had heard the story several times before and thought that he was drawing it out. He started in Bombay and worked his way, slowly up to Delhi and then Kathmandu before trekking all the way to Tibet. He had gone on a bit about the secret words of wisdom that the holy man was going to impart to him and we had just reached Llasa and had Holmes/Sigerson seated at the feet of the lama and the old man about to share his eternal words of wisdom when Holmes suddenly stopped in mid-sentence. He sputtered and coughed and raised his hand to his chest whilst his eyes rolled back. He stood up as if to run for the door and then staggered, dropped to one knee whilst grabbing the back of my chair, then he fell on the ground and convulsed.

"Get help!" I screamed. "One of you call for an ambulance. He has passed out!"

I leapt to my feet and dropped down to my knees beside him. I felt his pulse. It was still strong. I leaned my ear to listen for his breathing. Whilst my ear was within a quarter an inch of his nose and mouth I distinctly heard something I was not expecting.

"For heaven's sake, Watson. Faint. Now."

Ah ha, I thought to myself. I jumped back up to my feet.

"Get help," I shouted. I made as if to walk to the door and staggered, grabbing a chair for support. I staggered another step and grabbed another chair, then I fell onto my shoulder on the floor and rolled over onto my back. Being a doctor, I had seen hundreds of unconscious men over the years. So, I did my best. I rolled my eyes back into their sockets and blinked my eyelids irregularly. With a little effort, I worked up some saliva in my mouth and forced it out like froth. I thought I was quite convincing and apparently the folks at the table did as well.

"Well, tallyho and a-halloa," I heard Sir John saying. "Well done there, chaps. Well done. Do you agree, Gunga Din?"

"No," came the reply from the Indian. "It is very, very bad. He was about to tell us what the secret words were of the Lama. Now I shall never know. This is very, very bad."

"You will just have to get by without them, my boy. Now here, you grab Dr. Watson and I will drag Holmes, and we will get them next door."

I felt a strong pair of hands reach under my arms and start to drag my body across the floor and through the back door of the dining room. I was still rolling my eyes, which allowed me intermittent vision, and I could see that Sir John was doing the same with the limp body of Sherlock Holmes. There was a small flight of stairs leading to the back door and out into the alley. No care was taken to protect my legs and feet, and they bumped and banged rather uncomfortably down each step. Had I not been feigning, I might have shouted something to the effect of, "Do they not teach you how to move a body in medical schools in India?" but, given the circumstances, I refrained.

Next, I felt the fresh, bitter, cold night air of the alley as I was pulled along to the house next door.

"Wait here, *ladaka*," said Sir John. "I will get the lock."

I heard him drop Holmes's head and shoulders to the pavement and marveled at Holmes's resilience in just allowing it to happen. It would not have been pleasant. Not at all surprising, Sir John had the lock open in seconds. I was dragged into Camden House, through the kitchen and into the small room in which the bodies of Inspectors Jones and Forbes had been found. Then, my head and shoulders were unceremoniously dropped to the floor. Holmes endured the same fate and was deposited beside me. I could now account for the bumps on the back of the skulls of the two inspectors.

The door closed and I heard it locked. I was about to move and sit up when I felt the firm hand of Holmes on my forearm.

"Not yet," he whispered.

I lay still for a full ten minutes and then whispered, "Is it all right now?"

"Yes. But keep your voice down."

"What happens now?"

"They kill us."

"Lovely. How?"

"I do not know yet. We will have to wait and see."

"Well, please let me know before it happens," I said.

"I will do my best. I promise."

"I apologize," I said, "for not seeing that your fainting was a pretense. You were a bit dramatic, you know."

The stage had indeed lost a fine actor when Holmes gave up his theatrical aspirations.

"At least I did not start drooling," came the rejoinder.

"That is what men do when they are drugged into unconsciousness."

"If you say so, doctor. I prefer to keep saliva off my collar."

The two of us might have started to laugh at the absurdity of the situation had we not been worried about our ruse being discovered.

"How long do we have to wait?" I asked.

"Assuming that your diagnosis of the time of death of the other two was correct, I suspect it will be until morning. There was enough laudanum in that sherry to put a horse to sleep for an entire day. Somewhere past daybreak, they should murder us."

"How?"

"That is what we are about to find out, Watson. However, I do not recommend falling asleep. And keep your hand close to your revolver. You may need it."

"What if we need help?"

"Lestrade is sitting in the front room with two constables. There are three more in the back alley and three out on Baker Street."

"You truly are expecting something."

"They would not have gone this far just to leave us to wake up."

"They? So, it was not just Clay on his own."

"Correct."

I moved my body so that my back rested against a wall. I had enough foresight to put three small candles in my pocket and a box of Lucifers. In the dim glow, I could write up the events of the last few hours in my notebook before I was murdered.

We sat in the dark for a full eight hours. I managed to record everything I could remember of the events of this case so far and then went back to polish some of the other cases I had written in the recent past. The last candle was burned down to a stub when I looked at my watch and noted that it read six o'clock in the morning.

"Have they forgotten us, Holmes?"

"No, we are still alive. Patience, my friend."

My legs and backside had gone numb, and I stretched and stood up. I began to walk slowly and as quietly as I could around the small room.

"Stay still!" came Holmes's stage whisper.

"What for?"

"Listen!"

I did. At first, I heard nothing and then, very faintly, the sound of air swooshing. The noise appeared to be coming from the hearth.

Holmes crawled over to the hearth and gestured for me to follow him. He was passing his hands over the back bricking when he stopped.

"Here. Feel here."

He grabbed my wrist and moved my hand to a spot just below the flue plate. I could feel a strong current of very warm air. I leaned my head in and sniffed it.

"Good Lord. It is exhaust from a petrol engine."

"Clay's no doubt. They have started it up and attached a hose to the exhaust pipe and are forcing it through a chink in the brickwork. How very ingenious."

"But it has carbon monoxide in it," I said. "We will be dead in fifteen minutes in a small room like this. I am going to shout for Lestrade."

"No!" came the stage whisper command. "We cannot alarm them. If we do, they will be gone in a flash. They only have to clamber into the autocar and they will be long gone before we can apprehend them."

"Well then, let me get into the hearth and force the plate open with my feet and legs."

"No. They will hear us. Get over to the door. I will pick the lock," said Holmes.

On our hands and knees, we both moved silently to the door, and Holmes pulled out his small case of locksmith tools that he always carried. He had just started to work when my candle finally gave up the ghost and burned out.

"For goodness, sake, Holmes. We do not have much time."

"I am aware of that, doctor. We can get a gasp of fresh air by putting our noses to the base of the door. Clean air will be coming in from the other side."

I did as he suggested. There was not a breath of fresh air to be found.

"Ah, yes, of course," said Holmes. "They have laid a towel across the floor on the other side to block it. How very ingenious. That Clay fellow is quite the worthy adversary."

"Holmes, I do not give a tinker's cuss how clever he is. Quite frankly, I would not mind at all if you had his same skills in lock picking. We have only a few minutes left. I can feel myself getting dizzy now."

"Then take your belt off and use the stiff tongue to push the towel back."

I did so, and again dropped my nose to the floor and took a deep breath of the clean air seeping through under the door. Holmes stopped what he was doing and did the same. It took him several more minutes before he silently turned the door handle and opened it in complete silence.

"Come," he said. "We have to find Lestrade and slip back into Mrs. Turner's."

Without making a sound, we tiptoed through the house and alerted the inspector and his men. He, in turn, moved silently to find and alert the constables on Baker Street and in the alley.

Holmes then stealthily led Lestrade and two of his men into the back door of Mrs. Turner's house, and we stood in the kitchen. In the dining room, we could hear the voices of those with whom we had dinner.

"I trust you all slept well," I heard John Clay say cheerily. "Our task here is finished. Holmes, Watson and two of Scotland Yard's finest are dead and gone."

"I could have done it weeks ago if you hadda let me," growled a voice that I assigned to Mr. Tarker.

"Ah, Mr. Parker," said Clay. "Kindly remember that revenge is a dish best served cold. Your special garroting services would have been much too obvious and led Holmes directly to you. Our patience has been rewarded. As it was we ended up being rushed but the job is done. Would you agree, Dr. Roylott?"

"Yes, yes. But I do wish you had waited until Holmes told us what the Holy Lama had said."

"You are now free to go and ask him yourself. All you have to do is leave England and find your way to Tibet. And bon voyage," said Clay with a laugh.

"Now," continued Clay, "let us all be ladies and gentlemen and put the dear Mrs. Turner's dining room back in order, pack our bags and be gone before the poor old saint wakes up."

We could then hear some dishes being cleared and chairs being moved around.

"What the …!" came a loud exclamation from Clay.

"Bloody hell!" he was now shouting.

"*Was ist los*?"

"Look. Under their chairs!"

"*Was is es*?"

"On the carpet. On the carpet! Look. Two wet spots."

"So what?" said Mr. Parker. "Perhaps they had an accident, and bloody well pissed themselves."

"No! You fool. It's the sherry. They poured it out on the floor. It's a trap!"

Clay was now shouting.

"All of you. Into my car now. I'm leaving in one minute. If you are not in the vehicle, you can bloody well stay here and fend for yourself."

A second later, he crashed through the dining room door into the kitchen. He was met by five men, all with revolvers pointed at him.

"Good morning, John Clay," said Holmes. "We meet again."

Clay turned and tried to push his way back through the door.

"It is no use," said Holmes. "You have no chance at all. But I must compliment you. You took your revenge on Inspector Jones. Your automobile exhaust idea was very new and effective. And you, doctor," he said to the Indian chap, "a chip off the old block, are you not?"

The big fellow glared at Holmes. "You murdered my father. I have a right to kill you."

"Oh, come, come, doctor. Do I look like a swamp adder? And, my good inspector, allow me to introduce you to two women who also seem to not be very fond of either Scotland Yard or me. The woman who introduced herself to us as Alwyn Owen is actually the sensuous Miss Rachel Howells, at one time of the Musgrave estate. Many years ago, she was wronged by a butler named Brunston and avenged herself by subjecting him to a rather nasty and lonely end. I have been on her trail, relentlessly, now for thirty years.

"And the German lady, Princess Brunhilde, is rather angry at Scotland Yard and at me, and so is seeking her revenge."

"What in heaven's name for?" said Lestrade. "We are not at war with Germany, at least not yet."

"No, but this cold-hearted woman is the sister of Captain Franz Stark, currently employed by the German Legation and they have been continuing their father's plot to destroy Britain's economy by introducing millions of pounds of coined currency into circulation. She inherited her disposition from her father, Colonel Lysander Stark of the Kaiser's Imperial Guard. Your men caught up to him after he escaped from Eyford where he was pressing coinage. I believe that he swung for his crimes a few months back after you ignored the demands from Berlin for his extradition. It is a shame that his daughter has his ruthlessness in her blood and not the compassion of her mother. Would you not agree, Fräulein Stark?"

"*Fahr zur Hölle,*" was all the statuesque blonde woman said.

"And Mr. Parker, the Garrotter," said Holmes, looking at the small, furtive man. "You were here in the house quite recently were you not? Your loyalty to Professor Moriarty and your master, Colonel Moran, is remarkable if misguided. Both of them are now dead thanks to Scotland Yard and yours truly. Last time in this house, you escaped. Not this time though."

"You fiend. You clever fiend," Parker hissed in reply.

"Now, Inspector," said Holmes. "Whilst your men put the derbies on the lot of them, perhaps you will join Dr. Watson and me for a safe glass or two of sherry. Or perhaps brandy. Both are wonderful for the constitution."

Chapter Eight
In the Heart of All Men

O ur brief mood of exultation and celebration did not last long. By the time the three of us were seated in 221B Baker Street, a somber cloud had descended. Whilst justice had been served, we were forced to remember that two fine police inspectors had died and two families had been deprived of husbands and fathers.

Inspector Lestrade sat in silence for several minutes, sipping slowly on his sherry, before turning to Holmes.

"Well done, Holmes. Good work. Losing two of my best men is extremely upsetting. Thank you for acting so quickly. Well done. Might I ask when it was you deduced, as you say, that it was not just one killer behind the deaths, but all five of them?"

"That they were all using false identities was clear early on," said Holmes. "Inspector Forbes had discovered that. But that alone does not make a person suspect for murdering a police inspector. As I observed them and suspected the true identities of each of them, it occurred to me that all of them bore strong grudges against either me or Scotland Yard or both. The Indian doctor's true family name was confirmed late this afternoon by my contact in Calcutta. I had suspected that there might be a connection to Grimsby Roylott when Dr. Watson reported that the fellow had expertise in poisons, snake bites, and tropical ailments, and when he exhibited such an easy familiarity with Gypsies. He is his father's son in many ways. It is a shame, as he could have had an excellent medical career on Harley Street had blood not been thicker than water.

"I have been on the trail of Rachel Howells since the days when I was a student and invited down to Hurlstone by Reginald Musgrave thirty-five years ago. Back then, she was a lusty lover of a butler whom she did not hesitate to dispose of when he betrayed her affections. I was aware of the accounts of the deaths of two men who were the former husbands of a woman who now calls herself Mrs. Alwyn Owen."

"Yes," I interjected. "I recall those inquests. It was recorded that both husbands had suffered heart failure while in the throes of conjugal bliss, was it not?"

"It was," said Holmes. "I heard rumors that the coroners suspected that the old chaps may have been suffocated at a most inopportune time, leading to their heart attacks, but there was nothing that could be proved. Watching her confident and sensual familiarity with the men at the Criterion led me to connect her with the long-lost Rachel Howells.

"John Clay gave himself away both by his boasting, as reported by Mrs. Turner, of his royal blood and his uncanny skill as a criminal. I suspect that he would rather have postponed his plan for a while longer, but the ball was set rolling by the suspicions of the good Mrs. Turner and the diligent work of Inspector Forbes.

"The young German was an unknown entity until she greeted her brother. It was a simple task after that to learn the name of the young man working for the German Legation. As soon as I saw the name of Captain Stark on the directory, the connections all fell into place.

"Mr. Parker is simply not the sharpest knife in the drawer. Witness that he could not come up with a more clever disguising of his name than changing the first letter. Seeing that he was a paid criminal under contract to one of London's now most dangerous men suggested to me that he might be a killer for hire. I had seen him in the darkness when we surprised Colonel Moran in 222 Baker Street and even though I did not have a clear look at his face, his furtive and stealthy body movements were sufficiently similar to the garrotter Parker.

"Well now, Holmes, that is interesting, but not a full explanation," said Lestrade. "It only tells me that you had good reason to know that anyone of them might be the murderer."

Holmes gave the inspector a thin, sheepish smile. "I confess, that it was not until they all colluded over the dinner table that it dawned on me that the five of them had come together with the joint goal of murdering all of us. If you question them thoroughly, I expect that four of them will claim that it was John Clay who organized the series of events. He has the mind and the motive to do it."

"How would he have known about the others?" I asked.

"My dear Watson, it was thanks to you. He read all about them in the Strand. All he had to do was track down the appropriate parties and convince them to join his plot. And he almost got away with it."

It had not occurred to me that such might have been the unintended consequences of my setting Holmes's adventures to account. But another question vexed my spirit.

"But why, in heaven's name, would they go along with it and risk imprisonment or even the gallows?"

"Revenge."

"Revenge? Merely revenge?"

"My dear Watson, there is nothing *mere* about revenge. It has been one of the greatest forces for suffering, enmity, and death known to the human race throughout history. There may be the rare saint — our dear and recently departed Queen perhaps — whose heart is free of desires for revenge, but otherwise, it is an omnipresent evil. Over two thousand years ago, Thucydides informed us that under the euphemistic guise of honor, revenge was one of the universal causes of war. Homer reminded us that it launched a thousand ships.

Nothing has changed. Revenge has set brother against brother, village against village, and nation against nation. It festered like a cancer in these five people and when tempted with an opportunity to exact revenge, they yielded."

"But that is so utterly irrational."

"Rationality, my friend, has aught to do with it. A man may easily guard against the foolish decisions of his brain. I do so easily several times a day. It is in his heart and soul that a man succumbs to his evil desires. It is not without reason that Sir Francis told us that *a man that studieth revenge keeps his own wounds green.*

"Drake, the pirate, said *that?*" I asked.

"Please, Watson. Sir Francis Bacon."

A request to all readers:

After reading this story, please help the author and future readers by taking a moment to write a short, constructive review on the site from which you purchased the book. Thank you.   CSC

ALL New Sherlock Holmes Mysteries are FREE to borrow all the time on Kindle Unlimited/Prime.

Dear Sherlockian Reader:

On January 22, 1901, Queen Victoria died while staying at *Osborne House, her residence on the Isle of Wight. She had* ruled over the British Empire for sixty-three years, the longest of any British monarch until surpassed recently by Queen Elizabeth II.

Countless changes took place during the era of her reign, only a few of which I have noted in this story. The first automobiles appeared in England during the years immediately before the turn of the century.

The names and locations of various places in London that are mentioned in this story are accurate, with two exceptions. I stretched the date of the opening of the Piccadilly Hotel (now a Le Meridien) back a few years, as I also did with the opening of the Bakerloo Line of the Underground. The Metropolitan Line had been up and running for several years and was used by Alexander Holder when he came to see Holmes, as recorded in *The Adventure of the Beryl Coronet.*

The symptoms of asphyxiation by carbon monoxide are as described in the story.

The marriages and wives of Dr. Watson are a matter of longstanding debate among Sherlockians. Some scholars have argued that he was married up to six times. Many agree on three. And there are those of us who stick with one — the only one ever clearly recorded, Mary Morstan. Passing references in the stories to "my recent bereavement" or Watson's having "forsaken me for a wife" can be readily explained away without having to posit the existence of more wives and marriages.

Thank you for reading this New Sherlock Holmes Mystery. Hope you enjoyed it.

Warm regards,

Craig

About the Author

In May of 2014 the Sherlock Holmes Society of Canada –
better known as The Bootmakers – announced a contest for a
new Sherlock Holmes story. Although he had no experience
writing fiction, the author submitted a short Sherlock Holmes
mystery and was blessed to be declared one of the winners.
Thus inspired, he has continued to write new Sherlock Holmes
Mysteries since and is on a mission to write a new story as a
tribute to each of the sixty stories in the original Canon. He
currently writes from Toronto, the Okanagan, and Manhattan.
Several readers of New Sherlock Holmes Mysteries have
kindly sent him suggestions for future stories. You are
welcome to do likewise at craigstephencopland@gmail.com.

More Historical Mysteries
by Craig Stephen Copland

www.SherlockHolmesMystery.com

Copy the links to look inside and download

Studying Scarlet. Starlet O'Halloran, a fabulous mature woman, who reminds the reader of Scarlet O'Hara (but who, for copyright reasons cannot actually be her) has arrived in London looking for her long-lost husband, Brett (who resembles Rhett Butler, but who, for copyright reasons, cannot actually be him). She enlists the help of Sherlock Holmes. This is an unauthorized parody, inspired by Arthur Conan Doyle's *A Study in Scarlet* and Margaret Mitchell's *Gone with the Wind*. http://authl.it/aic

The Sign of the Third. Fifteen hundred years ago the courageous Princess Hemamali smuggled the sacred tooth of the Buddha into Ceylon. Now, for the first time, it is being brought to London to be part of a magnificent exhibit at the British Museum. But what if something were to happen to it? It would be a disaster for the British Empire. Sherlock Holmes, Dr. Watson, and even Mycroft Holmes are called upon to prevent such a crisis. This novella is inspired by the Sherlock Holmes mystery, *The Sign of the Four*. http://authl.it/aie

A Sandal from East Anglia. Archeological excavations at an old abbey unearth an ancient document that has the potential to change the course of the British Empire and all of Christendom. Holmes encounters some evil young men and a strikingly beautiful young Sister, with a curious double life. The mystery is inspired by the original Sherlock Holmes story, *A Scandal in Bohemia*. http://authl.it/aif

The Bald-Headed Trust. Watson insists on taking Sherlock Holmes on a short vacation to the seaside in Plymouth. No sooner has Holmes arrived than he is needed to solve a double murder and prevent a massive fraud diabolically designed by the evil Professor himself. Who knew that a family of devout conservative churchgoers could come to the aid of Sherlock Holmes and bring enormous grief to evil doers? The story is inspired by *The Red-Headed League*. http://authl.it/aih

A Case of Identity Theft. It is the fall of 1888 and Jack the Ripper is terrorizing London. A young married couple is found, minus their heads. Sherlock Holmes, Dr. Watson, the couple's mothers, and Mycroft must join forces to find the murderer before he kills again and makes off with half a million pounds. The novella is a tribute to *A Case of Identity*. It will appeal both to devoted fans of Sherlock Holmes, as well as to those who love the great game of rugby. http://authl.it/aii

The Hudson Valley Mystery. A young man in New York went mad and murdered his father. His mother believes he is innocent and knows he is not crazy. She appeals to Sherlock Holmes and, together with Dr. and Mrs. Watson, he crosses the Atlantic to help this client in need. This new story was inspired by *The Boscombe Valley Mystery*. http://authl.it/aij

The Mystery of the Five Oranges. A desperate father enters 221B Baker Street. His daughter has been kidnapped and spirited off to North America. The evil network who have taken her has spies everywhere. There is only one hope – Sherlock Holmes. Sherlockians will enjoy this new adventure, inspired by *The Five Orange Pips* and *Anne of Green Gables* http://authl.it/aik

. www.SherlockHolmesMystery.com

The Man Who Was Twisted But Hip. France is torn apart by The Dreyfus Affair. Westminster needs Sherlock Holmes so that the evil tide of anti-Semitism that has engulfed France will not spread. Sherlock and Watson go to Paris to solve the mystery and thwart Moriarty. This new mystery is inspired by, *The Man with the Twisted Lip,* as well as by *The Hunchback of Notre Dame.* http://authl.it/ail

The Adventure of the Blue Belt Buckle. A young street urchin discovers a man's belt and buckle under a bush in Hyde Park. A body is found in a hotel room in Mayfair. Scotland Yard seeks the help of Sherlock Holmes in solving the murder. The Queen's Jubilee could be ruined. Sherlock Holmes, Dr. Watson, Scotland Yard, and Her Majesty all team up to prevent a crime of unspeakable dimensions. A new mystery inspired by *The Blue Carbuncle.* http://authl.it/aim

The Adventure of the Spectred Bat. A beautiful young woman, just weeks away from giving birth, arrives at Baker Street in the middle of the night. Her sister was attacked by a bat and died, and now it is attacking her. A vampire? The story is a tribute to *The Adventure of the Speckled Band* and like the original, leaves the mind wondering and the heart racing. http://authl.it/ain

The Adventure of the Engineer's Mom. A brilliant young Cambridge University engineer is carrying out secret research for the Admiralty. It will lead to the building of the world's most powerful battleship, The Dreadnaught. His adventuress mother is kidnapped, and he seeks the help of Sherlock Holmes. This new mystery is a tribute to *The Engineer's Thumb*. http://authl.it/aio

The Adventure of the Notable Bachelorette. A snobbish nobleman enters 221B Baker Street demanding the help in finding his much younger wife – a beautiful and spirited American from the West. Three days later the wife is accused of a vile crime. Now she comes to Sherlock Holmes seeking to prove her innocence. This new mystery was inspired by *The Adventure of the Noble Bachelor*. http://authl.it/aip

The Adventure of the Beryl Anarchists. A deeply distressed banker enters 221B Baker St. His safe has been robbed, and he is certain that his motorcycle-riding sons have betrayed him. Highly incriminating and embarrassing records of the financial and personal affairs of England's nobility are now in the hands of blackmailers. Then a young girl is murdered. A tribute to *The Adventure of the Beryl Coronet*. http://authl.it/aiq

The Adventure of the Coiffured Bitches. A beautiful young woman will soon inherit a lot of money. She disappears. Another young woman finds out far too much and, in desperation seeks help. Sherlock Holmes, Dr. Watson and Miss Violet Hunter must solve the mystery of the coiffured bitches and avoid the massive mastiff that could tear their throats out. A tribute to *The Adventure of the Copper Beeches*. http://authl.it/air

The Silver Horse, Braised. The greatest horse race of the century will take place at Epsom Downs. Millions have been bet. Owners, jockeys, grooms, and gamblers from across England and America arrive. Jockeys and horses are killed. Holmes fails to solve the crime until... This mystery is a tribute to *Silver Blaze* and the great racetrack stories of Damon Runyon. http://authl.it/ais

The Box of Cards. A brother and a sister from a strict religious family disappear. The parents are alarmed, but Scotland Yard says they are just off sowing their wild oats. A horrific, gruesome package arrives in the post, and it becomes clear that a terrible crime is in process. Sherlock Holmes is called in to help. A tribute to *The Cardboard Box.* http://authl.it/ait

The Yellow Farce. Sherlock Holmes is sent to Japan. The war between Russia and Japan is raging. Alliances between countries in these years before World War I are fragile, and any misstep could plunge the world into Armageddon. The wife of the British ambassador is suspected of being a Russian agent. Join Holmes and Watson as they travel around the world to Japan. Inspired by *The Yellow Face.* http://authl.it/akp

The Stock Market Murders. A young man's friend has gone missing. Two more bodies of young men turn up. All are tied to The City and to one of the greatest frauds ever visited upon the citizens of England. The story is based on the true story of James Whitaker Wright and is inspired by, *The Stock Broker's Clerk.* Any resemblance of the villain to a certain American political figure is entirely coincidental. http://authl.it/akq

The Glorious Yacht. On the night of April 12, 1912, off the coast of Newfoundland, one of the greatest disasters of all time took place – the Unsinkable Titanic struck an iceberg and sank with a horrendous loss of life. The news of the disaster leads Holmes and Watson to reminisce about one of their earliest adventures. It began as a sailing race and ended as a tale of murder, kidnapping, piracy, and survival through a tempest. A tribute to *The Gloria Scott.* http://authl.it/akr

A Most Grave Ritual. In 1649, King Charles I escaped and made a desperate run for Continent. Did he leave behind a vast fortune? The patriarch of an ancient Royalist family dies in the courtyard, and the locals believe that the headless ghost of the king did him in. The police accuse his son of murder. Sherlock Holmes is hired to exonerate the lad. A tribute to *The Musgrave Ritual.* http://authl.it/aks

The Spy Gate Liars. Dr. Watson receives an urgent telegram telling him that Sherlock Holmes is in France and near death. He rushes to aid his dear friend, only to find that what began as a doctor's house call has turned into yet another adventure as Sherlock Holmes races to keep an unknown ruthless murderer from dispatching yet another former German army officer. A tribute to *The Reigate Squires.* http://authl.it/akt

The Cuckold Man Colonel James Barclay needs the help of Sherlock Holmes. His exceptionally beautiful, but much younger, wife has disappeared, and foul play is suspected. Has she been kidnapped and held for ransom? Or is she in the clutches of a deviant monster? The story is a tribute not only to the original mystery, *The Crooked Man*, but also to the biblical story of King David and Bathsheba. http://authl.it/akv

 **The Impatient Dissidents.** In March 1881, the Czar of Russia was assassinated by anarchists. That summer, an attempt was made to murder his daughter, Maria, the wife of England's Prince Alfred. A Russian Count is found dead in a hospital in London. Scotland Yard and the Home Office arrive at 221B and enlist the help of Sherlock Holmes to track down the killers and stop them. This new mystery is a tribute to *The Resident Patient.* http://authl.it/akw

 **The Grecian, Earned.** This story picks up where *The Greek Interpreter* left off. The villains of that story were murdered in Budapest, and so Holmes and Watson set off in search of "the Grecian girl" to solve the mystery. What they discover is a massive plot involving the re-birth of the Olympic games in 1896 and a colorful cast of characters at home and on the Continent. http://authl.it/aia

 **The Three Rhodes Not Taken.** Oxford University is famous for its passionate pursuit of learning. The Rhodes Scholarship has been recently established, and some men are prepared to lie, steal, slander, and, maybe murder, in the pursuit of it. Sherlock Holmes is called upon to track down a thief who has stolen vital documents pertaining to the winner of the scholarship, but what will he do when the prime suspect is found dead? A tribute to *The Three Students.* http://authl.it/al8

 **The Naval Knaves.** On September 15, 1894, an anarchist attempted to bomb the Greenwich Observatory. He failed, but the attempt led Sherlock Holmes into an intricate web of spies, foreign naval officers, and a beautiful princess. Once again, suspicion landed on poor Percy Phelps, now working in a senior position in the Admiralty, and once again Holmes has to use both his powers of deduction and raw courage to not only rescue Percy but to prevent an unspeakable disaster. A tribute to *The Naval Treaty.* http://authl.it/aia

A Scandal in Trumplandia. NOT a new mystery but a political satire. The story is a parody of the much-loved original story, *A Scandal in Bohemia*, with the character of the King of Bohemia replaced by you-know-who. If you enjoy both political satire and Sherlock Holmes, you will get a chuckle out of this new story. http://authl.it/aig

The Binomial Asteroid Problem. The deadly final encounter between Professor Moriarty and Sherlock Holmes took place at Reichenbach Falls. But when was their first encounter? This new story answers that question. What began a stolen Gladstone bag escalates into murder and more. This new story is a tribute to *The Adventure of the Final Problem.* http://authl.it/al1

The Adventure of Charlotte Europa Golderton. *Charles Augustus Milverton* was shot and sent to his just reward. But now another diabolical scheme of blackmail has emerged centered in the telegraph offices of the Royal Mail. It is linked to an archeological expedition whose director disappeared. Someone is prepared to murder to protect their ill-gotten gain and possibly steal a priceless treasure. Holmes is hired by not one but three women who need his help. http://authl.it/al7

The Mystery of 222 Baker Street. The body of a Scotland Yard inspector is found in a locked room in 222 Baker Street. There is no clue as to how he died, but he was murdered. Then another murder occurs in the very same room. Holmes and Watson might have to offer themselves as potential victims if the culprits are to be discovered. The story is a tribute to the original Sherlock Holmes story, *The Adventure of the Empty House.* http://authl.it/al3

The Adventure of the Norwood Rembrandt. A man facing execution appeals to Sherlock Holmes to save him. He claims that he is innocent. Holmes agrees to take on his case. Five years ago, he was convicted of the largest theft of art masterpieces in British history, and of murdering the butler who tried to stop him. Holmes and Watson have to find the real murderer and the missing works of art --- if the client is innocent after all. This new Sherlock Holmes mystery is a tribute to *The Adventure of the Norwood Builder* in the original Canon. http://authl.it/al4

The Horror of the Bastard's Villa. A Scottish clergyman and his faithful border collie visit 221B and tell a tale of a ghostly Banshee on the Isle of Skye. After the specter appeared, two people died. Holmes sends Watson on ahead to investigate and report. More terrifying horrors occur, and Sherlock Holmes must come and solve the awful mystery before more people are murdered. A tribute to the original story in the Canon, Arthur Conan Doyle's masterpiece, *The Hound of the Baskervilles.* http://authl.it/al2

The Dancer from the Dance. In 1909 the entire world of dance changed when Les Ballets Russes, under opened in Paris. They also made annual visits to the West End in London. Tragically, during their 1913 tour, two of their dancers are found murdered. Sherlock Holmes is brought into to find the murderer and prevent any more killings. The story adheres fairly closely to the history of ballet and is a tribute to the original story in the Canon, *The Adventure of the Dancing Men.* http://authl.it/al5

The Solitary Bicycle Thief. Remember Violet Smith, the beautiful young woman whom Sherlock Holmes and Dr. Watson rescued from a forced marriage, as recorded in *The Adventure of the Solitary Cyclist?* Ten years later she and Cyril reappear in 221B Baker Street with a strange tale of the theft of their bicycles. What on the surface seemed like a trifle turns out to be the door that leads Sherlock Holmes into a web of human trafficking, espionage, blackmail, and murder. A new and powerful cabal of master criminals has formed in London, and they will stop at nothing, not even the murder of an innocent foreign student, to extend the hold on the criminal underworld of London. http://authl.it/al6

The Adventure of the Prioress's Tale. The senior field hockey team from an elite girls' school goes to Dover for a beach holiday … and disappears. Have they been abducted into white slavery? Did they run off to Paris? Are they being held for ransom? Can Sherlock Holmes find them in time? Holmes, Watson, Lestrade, the Prioress of the school, and a new gang of Irregulars must find them before something terrible happens. A tribute to *The Adventure of the Priory School in the Canon.* http://authl.it/apr

The Adventure of Mrs. J.L. Heber. A mad woman is murdering London bachelors by driving a railway spike through their heads. Scotland Yard demands that Sherlock Holmes help them find and stop a crazed murderess who is re-enacting the biblical murders by Jael. Holmes agrees and finds that revenge is being taken for deeds treachery and betrayal that took place ten years ago in the Rocky Mountains of Canada. Holmes, Watson, and Lestrade must move quickly before more men and women lose their lives. The story is a tribute to the original Sherlock Holmes story, *The Adventure of Black Peter.* http://authl.it/arr

The Return of Napoleon. In October 1805, Napoleon's fleet was defeated in the Battle of Trafalgar. Now his ghost has returned to England for the centenary of the battle, intent on wreaking revenge on the descendants of Admiral Horatio Nelson and on all of England. The mother of the great-great-grandchildren of Admiral Nelson contacts Sherlock Holmes and asks him to come to her home, Victory Manor, in Gravesend to protect the Nelson Collection. The invaluable collection of artifacts is to be displayed during the one-hundredth anniversary celebrations of the Battle of Trafalgar. First, Dr. Watson comes to the manor and he meets not only the lovely children but also finds that something apparently supernatural is going on. Holmes assumes that some mad Frenchmen, intent on avenging Napoleon, are conspiring to wreak havoc on England and possibly threatening the children. Watson believes that something terrifying and occult may be at work. Neither is prepared for the true target of the Napoleonists, or of the Emperor's ghost. http://authl.it/at4

The Adventure of the Pinched Palimpsest. At Oxford University, an influential professor has been proselytizing for anarchism. Three naive students fall for his doctrines and decide to engage in direct action by stealing priceless artifacts from the British Museum, returning them to the oppressed people from whom their colonial masters stole them. In the midst of their caper, a museum guard is shot dead and they are charged with the murder. After being persuaded by a vulnerable friend of the students, Sherlock Holmes agrees to take on the case. He soon discovers that no one involved is telling the complete truth. Join Holmes and Watson as they race from London to Oxford, then to Cambridge and finally up to a remote village in Scotland and seek to discover the clues that are tied to an obscure medieval palimpsest. http://authl.it/ax0

. www.SherlockHolmesMystery.com

Contributions to
The Great Game of
Sherlockian Scholarship

Sherlock and Barack. This is NOT a new Sherlock Holmes Mystery. It is a Sherlockian research monograph. Why did Barack Obama win in November 2012? Why did Mitt Romney lose? Pundits and political scientists have offered countless reasons. This book reveals the truth - The Sherlock Holmes Factor. Had it not been for Sherlock Holmes, Mitt Romney would be president. http://authl.it/aid

From The Beryl Coronet to Vimy Ridge. This is NOT a New Sherlock Holmes Mystery. It is a monograph of Sherlockian research. This new monograph in the Great Game of Sherlockian scholarship argues that there was a Sherlock Holmes factor in the causes of World War I... and that it is secretly revealed in the *roman a clef* story that we know as *The Adventure of the Beryl Coronet.* http://authl.it/ali

Reverend Ezekiel Black—'The Sherlock Holmes of the American West'—Mystery Stories.

A Scarlet Trail of Murder. At ten o'clock on Sunday morning, the twenty-second of October, 1882, in an abandoned house in the West Bottom of Kansas City, a fellow named Jasper Harrison did not wake up. His inability to do was the result of his having had his throat cut. The Reverend Mr. Ezekiel Black, a part-time Methodist minister, and an itinerant US Marshall is called in. This original western mystery was inspired by the great Sherlock Holmes classic, *A Study in Scarlet.* http://authl.it/alg

The Brand of the Flying Four. This case all began one quiet evening in a room in Kansas City. A few weeks later, a gruesome murder, took place in Denver. By the time Rev. Black had solved the mystery, justice, of the frontier variety, not the courtroom, had been meted out. The story is inspired by *The Sign of the Four* by Arthur Conan Doyle, and like that story, it combines murder most foul, and romance most enticing. http://authl.it/alh

www.SherlockHolmesMystery.com

Collection Sets for eBooks and paperback are available at *40% off the price of buying them separately.*

Collection One http://authl.it/al9
The Sign of the Tooth
The Hudson Valley Mystery
A Case of Identity Theft
The Bald-Headed Trust
Studying Scarlet
The Mystery of the Five Oranges

Collection Two http://authl.it/ala
A Sandal from East Anglia
The Man Who Was Twisted But Hip
The Blue Belt Buckle
The Spectred Bat

Collection Three http://authl.it/alb
The Engineer's Mom
The Notable Bachelorette
The Beryl Anarchists
The Coiffured Bitches

Collection Four http://authl.it/alc

The Silver Horse, Braised
The Box of Cards
The Yellow Farce
The Three Rhodes Not Taken

Collection Five http://authl.it/ald

The Stock Market Murders
The Glorious Yacht
The Most Grave Ritual
The Spy Gate Liars

Collection Six http://authl.it/ale

The Cuckold Man
The Impatient Dissidents
The Grecian, Earned
The Naval Knaves

Collection Seven http://authl.it/alf

The Binomial Asteroid Problem
The Mystery of 222 Baker Street
The Adventure of Charlotte Europa Golderton
The Adventure of the Norwood Rembrandt

Collection Eight http://authl.it/at3

The Dancer from the Dance
The Adventure of the Prioress's Tale
The Adventure of Mrs. J. L. Heber
The Solitary Bicycle Thief

Super Collections A and B

30 New Sherlock Holmes Mysteries.

The perfect ebooks for readers who can only borrow one book a month from Amazon

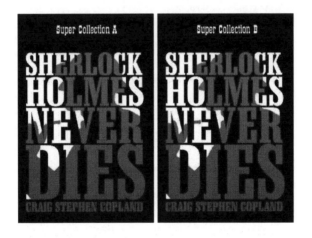

www.SherlockHolmesMystery.com

The Adventure of the Empty House

The Original Sherlock Holmes Story

Arthur Conan Doyle

The Adventure
of the Empty House

It was in the spring of the year 1894 that all London was interested, and the fashionable world dismayed, by the murder of the Honourable Ronald Adair under most unusual and inexplicable circumstances. The public has already learned those particulars of the crime which came out in the police investigation; but a good deal was suppressed upon that occasion, since the case for the prosecution was so overwhelmingly strong that it was not necessary to bring forward all the facts. Only now, at the end of nearly ten years, am I allowed to supply those missing links which make up the whole of that remarkable chain. The crime was of interest in itself, but that interest was as nothing to me compared to the inconceivable sequel, which afforded me the greatest shock and surprise of any event in my adventurous life. Even now, after this long interval, I find myself thrilling as I think of it, and feeling once more that sudden flood of joy, amazement, and incredulity which utterly submerged my mind. Let me say to that public which has shown some interest in those glimpses which I have occasionally given them of the thoughts and actions of a very remarkable man that they are not to blame me if I have not shared my knowledge with them, for I should have considered it my first duty to have done so had I not been barred by a positive prohibition from his own lips, which was only withdrawn upon the third of last month.

It can be imagined that my close intimacy with Sherlock Holmes had interested me deeply in crime, and that after his disappearance I never failed to read with care the various problems which came before the public, and I even attempted more than once for my own private satisfaction to employ his methods in their solution, though with indifferent success. There was none, however, which appealed to me like this tragedy of Ronald Adair. As I read the evidence at the inquest, which led up to a verdict of willful murder against some person or persons, I realized more clearly than I had ever done the loss which the community had sustained by the death of Sherlock Holmes. There were points about this strange business which would, I was sure, have specially appealed to him, and the efforts of the police would have been supplemented, or more probably anticipated, by the trained observation and the alert mind of the first criminal agent in Europe. All day as I drove upon my round I turned over the case in my mind, and found no explanation which appeared to me to be adequate. At the risk of telling a twice-told tale, I will recapitulate the facts as they were known to the public at the conclusion of the inquest.

The Honourable Ronald Adair was the second son of the Earl of Maynooth, at that time Governor of one of the Australian Colonies. Adair's mother had returned from Australia to undergo the operation for cataract, and she, her son Ronald, and her daughter Hilda were living together at 427, Park Lane. The youth moved in the best society, had, so far as was known, no enemies, and no particular vices. He had been engaged to Miss Edith Woodley, of Carstairs, but the engagement had been broken off by mutual consent some months before, and there was no sign that it had left any very profound feeling behind it. For the rest the man's life moved in a narrow and conventional circle, for his habits were quiet and his nature unemotional. Yet it was upon this easy-going young aristocrat that death came in most strange and unexpected form between the hours of ten and eleven-twenty on the night of March 30, 1894.

Ronald Adair was fond of cards, playing continually, but never for such stakes as would hurt him. He was a member of the Baldwin, the Cavendish, and the Bagatelle card clubs. It was shown that after dinner on the day of his death he had played a rubber of whist at the latter club. He had also played there in the afternoon. The evidence of those who had played with him —Mr. Murray, Sir John Hardy, and Colonel Moran—showed that the game was whist, and that there was a fairly equal fall of the cards. Adair might have lost five pounds, but not more. His fortune was a considerable one, and such a loss could not in any way affect him. He had played nearly every day at one club or other, but he was a cautious player, and usually rose a winner. It came out in evidence that in partnership with Colonel Moran he had actually won as much as four hundred and twenty pounds in a sitting some weeks before from Godfrey Milner and Lord Balmoral. So much for his recent history, as it came out at the inquest.

On the evening of the crime, he returned from the club exactly at ten. His mother and sister were out spending the evening with a relation. The servant deposed that she heard him enter the front room on the second floor, generally used as his sitting-room. She had lit a fire there, and as it smoked, she had opened the window. No sound was heard from the room until eleven-twenty, the hour of the return of Lady Maynooth and her daughter. Desiring to say good-night, she had attempted to enter her son's room. The door was locked on the inside, and no answer could be got to their cries and knocking. Help was obtained, and the door forced. The unfortunate young man was found lying near the table. His head had been horribly mutilated by an expanding revolver bullet, but no weapon of any sort was to be found in the room. On the table lay two bank-notes for ten pounds each and seventeen pounds ten in silver and gold, the money arranged in little piles of varying amount. There were some figures also upon a sheet of paper with the names of some club friends opposite to them, from which it was conjectured that before his death he was endeavouring to make out his losses or winnings at cards.

A minute examination of the circumstances served only to make the case more complex. In the first place, no reason could be given why the young man should have fastened the door upon the inside. There was the possibility that the murderer had done this and had afterwards escaped by the window. The drop was at least twenty feet, however, and a bed of crocuses in full bloom lay beneath. Neither the flowers nor the earth showed any sign of having been disturbed, nor were there any marks upon the narrow strip of grass which separated the house from the road. Apparently, therefore, it was the young man himself who had fastened the door. But how did he come by his death? No one could have climbed up to the window without leaving traces. Suppose a man had fired through the window, it would indeed be a remarkable shot who could with a revolver inflict so deadly a wound. Again, Park Lane is a frequented thoroughfare, and there is a cab-stand within a hundred yards of the house. No one had heard a shot. And yet there was the dead man, and there the revolver bullet, which had mushroomed out, as soft-nosed bullets will, and so inflicted a wound which must have caused instantaneous death. Such were the circumstances of the Park Lane Mystery, which were further complicated by entire absence of motive, since, as I have said, young Adair was not known to have any enemy, and no attempt had been made to remove the money or valuables in the room.

All day I turned these facts over in my mind, endeavouring to hit upon some theory which could reconcile them all, and to find that line of least resistance which my poor friend had declared to be the starting-point of every investigation. I confess that I made little progress. In the evening I strolled across the Park, and found myself about six o'clock at the Oxford Street end of Park Lane. A group of loafers upon the pavements, all staring up at a particular window, directed me to the house which I had come to see. A tall, thin man with coloured glasses, whom I strongly suspected of being a plain-clothes detective, was pointing out some theory of his own, while the others crowded round to listen to what he said. I got as near him as I could, but his observations seemed to me to be absurd, so I withdrew again in some disgust. As I did so I struck against an elderly deformed man, who had been behind me, and I knocked down several books which he was carrying. I remember that as I picked them up I observed the title of one of them, "The Origin of Tree Worship," and it struck me that the fellow must be some poor bibliophile who, either as a trade or as a hobby, was a collector of obscure volumes. I endeavoured to apologize for the accident, but it was evident that these books which I had so unfortunately maltreated were very precious objects in the eyes of their owner. With a snarl of contempt, he turned upon his heel, and I saw his curved back and white side-whiskers disappear among the throng.

My observations of No. 427, Park Lane did little to clear up the problem in which I was interested. The house was separated from the street by a low wall and railing, the whole not more than five feet high. It was perfectly easy, therefore, for anyone to get into the garden, but the window was entirely inaccessible, since there was no water-pipe or anything which could help the most active man to climb it. More puzzled than ever I retraced my steps to Kensington. I had not been in my study five minutes when the maid entered to say that a person desired to see me. To my astonishment it was none other than my strange old book-collector, his sharp, wizened face peering out from a frame of white hair, and his precious volumes, a dozen of them at least, wedged under his right arm.

"You're surprised to see me, sir," said he, in a strange, croaking voice.

I acknowledged that I was.

"Well, I've a conscience, sir, and when I chanced to see you go into this house, as I came hobbling after you, I thought to myself, I'll just step in and see that kind gentleman, and tell him that if I was a bit gruff in my manner there was not any harm meant, and that I am much obliged to him for picking up my books."

"You make too much of a trifle," said I. "May I ask how you knew who I was?"

"Well, sir, if it isn't too great a liberty, I am a neighbour of yours, for you'll find my little bookshop at the corner of Church Street, and very happy to see you, I am sure. Maybe you collect yourself, sir; here's 'British Birds,' and 'Catullus,' and 'The Holy War'—a bargain every one of them. With five volumes you could just fill that gap on that second shelf. It looks untidy, does it not, sir?"

I moved my head to look at the cabinet behind me. When I turned again Sherlock Holmes was standing smiling at me across my study table. I rose to my feet, stared at him for some seconds in utter amazement, and then it appears that I must have fainted for the first and the last time in my life. Certainly a grey mist swirled before my eyes, and when it cleared I found my collar-ends undone and the tingling after-taste of brandy upon my lips. Holmes was bending over my chair, his flask in his hand.

"My dear Watson," said the well-remembered voice, "I owe you a thousand apologies. I had no idea that you would be so affected."

I gripped him by the arm.

"Holmes!" I cried. "Is it really you? Can it indeed be that you are alive? Is it possible that you succeeded in climbing out of that awful abyss?"

"Wait a moment," said he. "Are you sure that you are really fit to discuss things? I have given you a serious shock by my unnecessarily dramatic reappearance."

"I am all right, but indeed, Holmes, I can hardly believe my eyes. Good heavens, to think that you—you of all men— should be standing in my study!" Again I gripped him by the sleeve and felt the thin, sinewy arm beneath it. "Well, you're not a spirit, anyhow," said I. "My dear chap, I am overjoyed to see you. Sit down and tell me how you came alive out of that dreadful chasm."

He sat opposite to me and lit a cigarette in his old nonchalant manner. He was dressed in the seedy frock-coat of the book merchant, but the rest of that individual lay in a pile of white hair and old books upon the table. Holmes looked even thinner and keener than of old, but there was a dead-white tinge in his aquiline face which told me that his life recently had not been a healthy one.

"I am glad to stretch myself, Watson," said he. "It is no joke when a tall man has to take a foot off his stature for several hours on end. Now, my dear fellow, in the matter of these explanations we have, if I may ask for your co-operation, a hard and dangerous night's work in front of us. Perhaps it would be better if I gave you an account of the whole situation when that work is finished."

"I am full of curiosity. I should much prefer to hear now."

"You'll come with me to-night?"

"When you like and where you like."

"This is indeed like the old days. We shall have time for a mouthful of dinner before we need go. Well, then, about that chasm. I had no serious difficulty in getting out of it, for the very simple reason that I never was in it."

"You never were in it?"

"No, Watson, I never was in it. My note to you was absolutely genuine. I had little doubt that I had come to the end of my career when I perceived the somewhat sinister figure of the late Professor Moriarty standing upon the narrow pathway which led to safety. I read an inexorable purpose in his grey eyes. I exchanged some remarks with him, therefore, and obtained his courteous permission to write the short note which you afterwards received. I left it with my cigarette-box and my stick and I walked along the pathway, Moriarty still at my heels. When I reached the end, I stood at bay. He drew no weapon, but he rushed at me and threw his long arms around me. He knew that his own game was up, and was only anxious to revenge himself upon me. We tottered together upon the brink of the fall. I have some knowledge, however, of baritsu, or the Japanese system of wrestling, which has more than once been very useful to me. I slipped through his grip, and he with a horrible scream kicked madly for a few seconds and clawed the air with both his hands. But for all his efforts he could not get his balance, and over he went. With my face over the brink I saw him fall for a long way. Then he struck a rock, bounded off, and splashed into the water."

I listened with amazement to this explanation, which Holmes delivered between the puffs of his cigarette.

"But the tracks!" I cried. "I saw with my own eyes that two went down the path and none returned."

"It came about in this way. The instant that the Professor had disappeared it struck me what a really extraordinarily lucky chance Fate had placed in my way. I knew that Moriarty was not the only man who had sworn my death. There were at least three others whose desire for vengeance upon me would only be increased by the death of their leader. They were all most dangerous men. One or other would certainly get me. On the other hand, if all the world was convinced that I was dead they would take liberties, these men, they would lay themselves open, and sooner or later I could destroy them. Then it would be time for me to announce that I was still in the land of the living. So rapidly does the brain act that I believe I had thought this all out before Professor Moriarty had reached the bottom of the Reichenbach Fall.

"I stood up and examined the rocky wall behind me. In your picturesque account of the matter, which I read with great interest some months later, you assert that the wall was sheer. This was not literally true. A few small footholds presented themselves, and there was some indication of a ledge. The cliff is so high that to climb it all was an obvious impossibility, and it was equally impossible to make my way along the wet path without leaving some tracks. I might, it is true, have reversed my boots, as I have done on similar occasions, but the sight of three sets of tracks in one direction would certainly have suggested a deception. On the whole, then, it was best that I should risk the climb. It was not a pleasant business, Watson. The fall roared beneath me. I am not a fanciful person, but I give you my word that I seemed to hear Moriarty's voice screaming at me out of the abyss. A mistake would have been fatal. More than once, as tufts of grass came out in my hand or my foot slipped in the wet notches of the rock, I thought that I was gone. But I struggled upwards, and at last I reached a ledge several feet deep and covered with soft green moss, where I could lie unseen in the most perfect comfort. There I was stretched when you, my dear Watson, and all your following were investigating in the most sympathetic and inefficient manner the circumstances of my death.

"At last, when you had all formed your inevitable and totally erroneous conclusions, you departed for the hotel and I was left alone. I had imagined that I had reached the end of my adventures, but a very unexpected occurrence showed me that there were surprises still in store for me. A huge rock, falling from above, boomed past me, struck the path, and bounded over into the chasm. For an instant I thought that it was an accident; but a moment later, looking up, I saw a man's head against the darkening sky, and another stone struck the very ledge upon which I was stretched, within a foot of my head. Of course, the meaning of this was obvious. Moriarty had not been alone. A confederate—and even that one glance had told me how dangerous a man that confederate was— had kept guard while the Professor had attacked me. From a distance, unseen by me, he had been a witness of his friend's death and of my escape. He had waited, and then, making his way round to the top of the cliff, he had endeavoured to succeed where his comrade had failed.

"I did not take long to think about it, Watson. Again I saw that grim face look over the cliff, and I knew that it was the precursor of another stone. I scrambled down on to the path. I don't think I could have done it in cold blood. It was a hundred times more difficult than getting up. But I had no time to think of the danger, for another stone sang past me as I hung by my hands from the edge of the ledge. Halfway down I slipped, but by the blessing of God I landed, torn and bleeding, upon the path. I took to my heels, did ten miles over the mountains in the darkness, and a week later I found myself in Florence with the certainty that no one in the world knew what had become of me.

"I had only one confidant—my brother Mycroft. I owe you many apologies, my dear Watson, but it was all-important that it should be thought I was dead, and it is quite certain that you would not have written so convincing an account of my unhappy end had you not yourself thought that it was true. Several times during the last three years I have taken up my pen to write to you, but always I feared lest your affectionate regard for me should tempt you to some indiscretion which would betray my secret. For that reason, I turned away from you this evening when you upset my books, for I was in danger at the time, and any show of surprise and emotion upon your part might have drawn attention to my identity and led to the most deplorable and irreparable results. As to Mycroft, I had to confide in him in order to obtain the money which I needed. The course of events in London did not run so well as I had hoped, for the trial of the Moriarty gang left two of its most dangerous members, my own most vindictive enemies, at liberty. I traveled for two years in Tibet, therefore, and amused myself by visiting Lhassa and spending some days with the head Llama. You may have read of the remarkable explorations of a Norwegian named Sigerson, but I am sure that it never occurred to you that you were receiving news of your friend. I then passed through Persia, looked in at Mecca, and paid a short but interesting visit to the Khalifa at Khartoum, the results of which I have communicated to the Foreign Office. Returning to France I spent some months in a research into the coal-tar derivatives, which I conducted in a laboratory at Montpelier, in the South of France. Having concluded this to my satisfaction, and learning that only one of my enemies was now left in London, I was about to return when my movements were hastened by the news of this very remarkable Park Lane Mystery, which not only appealed to me by its own merits, but which seemed to offer some most peculiar personal opportunities. I came over at once to London, called in my own person at Baker

Street, threw Mrs. Hudson into violent hysterics, and found that Mycroft had preserved my rooms and my papers exactly as they had always been. So it was, my dear Watson, that at two o'clock to-day I found myself in my old arm-chair in my own old room, and only wishing that I could have seen my old friend Watson in the other chair which he has so often adorned."

Such was the remarkable narrative to which I listened on that April evening—a narrative which would have been utterly incredible to me had it not been confirmed by the actual sight of the tall, spare figure and the keen, eager face, which I had never thought to see again. In some manner he had learned of my own sad bereavement, and his sympathy was shown in his manner rather than in his words. "Work is the best antidote to sorrow, my dear Watson," said he, "and I have a piece of work for us both to-night which, if we can bring it to a successful conclusion, will in itself justify a man's life on this planet." In vain I begged him to tell me more. "You will hear and see enough before morning," he answered. "We have three years of the past to discuss. Let that suffice until half-past nine, when we start upon the notable adventure of the empty house."

It was indeed like old times when, at that hour, I found myself seated beside him in a hansom, my revolver in my pocket and the thrill of adventure in my heart. Holmes was cold and stern and silent. As the gleam of the street-lamps flashed upon his austere features I saw that his brows were drawn down in thought and his thin lips compressed. I knew not what wild beast we were about to hunt down in the dark jungle of criminal London, but I was well assured from the bearing of this master huntsman that the adventure was a most grave one, while the sardonic smile which occasionally broke through his ascetic gloom boded little good for the object of our quest.

I had imagined that we were bound for Baker Street, but Holmes stopped the cab at the corner of Cavendish Square. I observed that as he stepped out he gave a most searching glance to right and left, and at every subsequent street corner he took the utmost pains to assure that he was not followed. Our route was certainly a singular one. Holmes's knowledge of the byways of London was extraordinary, and on this occasion he passed rapidly, and with an assured step, through a network of mews and stables the very existence of which I had never known. We emerged at last into a small road, lined with old, gloomy houses, which led us into Manchester Street, and so to Blandford Street. Here he turned swiftly down a narrow passage, passed through a wooden gate into a deserted yard, and then opened with a key the back door of a house. We entered together and he closed it behind us.

The place was pitch-dark, but it was evident to me that it was an empty house. Our feet creaked and crackled over the bare planking, and my outstretched hand touched a wall from which the paper was hanging in ribbons. Holmes's cold, thin fingers closed round my wrist and led me forwards down a long hall, until I dimly saw the murky fanlight over the door. Here Holmes turned suddenly to the right, and we found ourselves in a large, square, empty room, heavily shadowed in the corners, but faintly lit in the centre from the lights of the street beyond. There was no lamp near and the window was thick with dust, so that we could only just discern each other's figures within. My companion put his hand upon my shoulder and his lips close to my ear.

"Do you know where we are?" he whispered.

"Surely that is Baker Street," I answered, staring through the dim window.

"Exactly. We are in Camden House, which stands opposite to our own old quarters."

"But why are we here?"

"Because it commands so excellent a view of that picturesque pile. Might I trouble you, my dear Watson, to draw a little nearer to the window, taking every precaution not to show yourself, and then to look up at our old rooms— the starting-point of so many of our little adventures? We will see if my three years of absence have entirely taken away my power   to   surprise   you."
a house

I crept forward and looked across at the familiar window. As my eyes fell upon it I gave a gasp and a cry of amazement. The blind was down and a strong light was burning in the room. The shadow of a man who was seated in a chair within was thrown in hard, black outline upon the luminous screen of the window. There was no mistaking the poise of the head, the squareness of the shoulders, the sharpness of the features. The face was turned half-round, and the effect was that of one of those black silhouettes which our grandparents loved to frame. It was a perfect reproduction of Holmes. So amazed was I that I threw out my hand to make sure that the man himself was standing beside me. He was quivering with silent laughter.

"Well?" said he.

"Good heavens!" I cried. "It is marvelous."

"I trust that age doth not wither nor custom stale my infinite variety,'" said he, and I recognized in his voice the joy and pride which the artist takes in his own creation. "It really is rather like me, is it not?"

"I should be prepared to swear that it was you."

"The credit of the execution is due to Monsieur Oscar Meunier, of Grenoble, who spent some days in doing the moulding. It is a bust in wax. The rest I arranged myself during my visit to Baker Street this afternoon."

"But why?"

"Because, my dear Watson, I had the strongest possible reason for wishing certain people to think that I was there when I was really elsewhere."

"And you thought the rooms were watched?"

"I KNEW that they were watched."

"By whom?"

"By my old enemies, Watson. By the charming society whose leader lies in the Reichenbach Fall. You must remember that they knew, and only they knew, that I was still alive. Sooner or later they believed that I should come back to my rooms. They watched them continuously, and this morning they saw me arrive."

"How do you know?"

"Because I recognized their sentinel when I glanced out of my window. He is a harmless enough fellow, Parker by name, a garroter by trade, and a remarkable performer upon the Jew's harp. I cared nothing for him. But I cared a great deal for the much more formidable person who was behind him, the bosom friend of Moriarty, the man who dropped the rocks over the cliff, the most cunning and dangerous criminal in London. That is the man who is after me to-night, Watson, and that is the man who is quite unaware that we are after HIM."

My friend's plans were gradually revealing themselves. From this convenient retreat the watchers were being watched and the trackers tracked. That angular shadow up yonder was the bait and we were the hunters. In silence we stood together in the darkness and watched the hurrying figures who passed and repassed in front of us. Holmes was silent and motionless; but I could tell that he was keenly alert, and that his eyes were fixed intently upon the stream of passers-by. It was a bleak and boisterous night, and the wind whistled shrilly down the long street. Many people were moving to and fro, most of them muffled in their coats and cravats. Once or twice it seemed to me that I had seen the same figure before, and I especially noticed two men who appeared to be sheltering themselves from the wind in the doorway of a house some distance up the street. I tried to draw my companion's attention to them, but he gave a little ejaculation of impatience and continued to stare into the street. More than once he fidgeted with his feet and tapped rapidly with his fingers upon the wall. It was evident to me that he was becoming uneasy and that his plans were not working out altogether as he had hoped. At last, as midnight approached and the street gradually cleared, he paced up and down the room in uncontrollable agitation. I was about to make some remark to him when I raised my eyes to the lighted window and again experienced almost as great a surprise as before. I clutched Holmes's arm and pointed upwards.

"The shadow has moved!" I cried.

It was, indeed, no longer the profile, but the back, which was turned towards us.

Three years had certainly not smoothed the asperities of his temper or his impatience with a less active intelligence than his own.

"Of course it has moved," said he. "Am I such a farcical bungler, Watson, that I should erect an obvious dummy and expect that some of the sharpest men in Europe would be deceived by it? We have been in this room two hours, and Mrs. Hudson has made some change in that figure eight times, or once in every quarter of an hour. She works it from the front so that her shadow may never be seen. Ah!" He drew in his breath with a shrill, excited intake. In the dim light I saw his head thrown forward, his whole attitude rigid with attention. Outside, the street was absolutely deserted. Those two men might still be crouching in the doorway, but I could no longer see them. All was still and dark, save only that brilliant yellow screen in front of us with the black figure outlined upon its centre. Again in the utter silence I heard that thin, sibilant note which spoke of intense suppressed excitement. An instant later he pulled me back into the blackest corner of the room, and I felt his warning hand upon my lips. The fingers which clutched me were quivering. Never had I known my friend more moved, and yet the dark street still stretched lonely and motionless before us.

But suddenly I was aware of that which his keener senses had already distinguished. A low, stealthy sound came to my ears, not from the direction of Baker Street, but from the back of the very house in which we lay concealed. A door opened and shut. An instant later steps crept down the passage— steps which were meant to be silent, but which reverberated harshly through the empty house. Holmes crouched back against the wall and I did the same, my hand closing upon the handle of my revolver. Peering through the gloom, I saw the vague outline of a man, a shade blacker than the blackness of the open door. He stood for an instant, and then he crept forward, crouching, menacing, into the room. He was within three yards of us, this sinister figure, and I had braced myself to meet his spring, before I realized that he had no idea of our presence. He passed close beside us, stole over to the window, and very softly and noiselessly raised it for half a foot. As he sank to the level of this opening the light of the street, no longer dimmed by the dusty glass, fell full upon his face. The man seemed to be beside himself with excitement. His two eyes shone like stars and his features were working convulsively. He was an elderly man, with a thin, projecting nose, a high, bald forehead, and a huge grizzled moustache. An opera-hat was pushed to the back of his head, and an evening dress shirt-front gleamed out through his open overcoat. His face was gaunt and swarthy, scored with deep, savage lines. In his hand he carried what appeared to be a stick, but as he laid it down upon the floor it gave a metallic clang. Then from the pocket of his overcoat he drew a bulky object, and he busied himself in some task which ended with a loud, sharp click, as if a spring or bolt had fallen into its place. Still kneeling upon the floor, he bent forward and threw all his weight and strength upon some lever, with the result that there came a long, whirling, grinding noise, ending once more in a powerful click. He straightened himself then, and I saw that what he held in his hand was a sort of gun, with a curiously misshapen butt. He opened it at the breech, put something in, and snapped the breech-block. Then, crouching down, he rested the end of the barrel upon the ledge of the open window, and I saw his long moustache droop over the stock and his eye gleam as it peered along the sights. I heard a little sigh of satisfaction as he cuddled the butt into his shoulder, and saw that amazing target, the black man on the yellow ground, standing clear at the end of his fore sight. For an instant he was rigid and motionless. Then his finger tightened on the trigger. There was a strange, loud whiz and a long, silvery tinkle of broken glass. At that instant Holmes sprang like a tiger on to the marksman's back and hurled him flat upon his face. He was up again in a moment, and with convulsive strength he seized Holmes by the throat; but I struck him on the head with the butt of my revolver and he dropped again upon the floor. I fell upon him, and as I held him my comrade blew a shrill call upon a whistle. There was the clatter of running feet upon the pavement, and two policemen in uniform, with one plain-clothes detective, rushed through the front entrance and into the room.

"That you, Lestrade?" said Holmes.

"Yes, Mr. Holmes. I took the job myself. It's good to see you back in London, sir."

"I think you want a little unofficial help. Three undetected murders in one year won't do, Lestrade. But you handled the Molesey Mystery with less than your usual—that's to say, you handled it fairly well."

We had all risen to our feet, our prisoner breathing hard, with a stalwart constable on each side of him. Already a few loiterers had begun to collect in the street. Holmes stepped up to the window, closed it, and dropped the blinds. Lestrade had produced two candles and the policemen had uncovered their lanterns. I was able at last to have a good look at our prisoner.

It was a tremendously virile and yet sinister face which was turned towards us. With the brow of a philosopher above and the jaw of a sensualist below, the man must have started with great capacities for good or for evil. But one could not look upon his cruel blue eyes, with their drooping, cynical lids, or upon the fierce, aggressive nose and the threatening, deep-lined brow, without reading Nature's plainest danger-signals. He took no heed of any of us, but his eyes were fixed upon Holmes's face with an expression in which hatred and amazement were equally blended. "You fiend!" he kept on muttering. "You clever, clever fiend!"

"Ah, Colonel!" said Holmes, arranging his rumpled collar; "'journeys end in lovers' meetings,' as the old play says. I don't think I have had the pleasure of seeing you since you favoured me with those attentions as I lay on the ledge above the Reichenbach Fall."

The Colonel still stared at my friend like a man in a trance. "You cunning, cunning fiend!" was all that he could say.

"I have not introduced you yet," said Holmes. "This, gentlemen, is Colonel Sebastian Moran, once of Her Majesty's Indian Army, and the best heavy game shot that our Eastern Empire has ever produced. I believe I am correct, Colonel, in saying that your bag of tigers still remains unrivalled?"

The fierce old man said nothing, but still glared at my companion; with his savage eyes and bristling moustache he was wonderfully like a tiger himself.

"I wonder that my very simple stratagem could deceive so old a shikari," said Holmes. "It must be very familiar to you. Have you not tethered a young kid under a tree, lain above it with your rifle, and waited for the bait to bring up your tiger? This empty house is my tree and you are my tiger. You have possibly had other guns in reserve in case there should be several tigers, or in the unlikely supposition of your own aim failing you. These," he pointed around, "are my other guns. The parallel is exact."

Colonel Moran sprang forward, with a snarl of rage, but the constables dragged him back. The fury upon his face was terrible to look at.

"I confess that you had one small surprise for me," said Holmes. "I did not anticipate that you would yourself make use of this empty house and this convenient front window. I had imagined you as operating from the street, where my friend Lestrade and his merry men were awaiting you. With that exception all has gone as I expected."

Colonel Moran turned to the official detective.

"You may or may not have just cause for arresting me," said he, "but at least there can be no reason why I should submit to the gibes of this person. If I am in the hands of the law let things be done in a legal way."

"Well, that's reasonable enough," said Lestrade. "Nothing further you have to say, Mr. Holmes, before we go?"

Holmes had picked up the powerful air-gun from the floor and was examining its mechanism.

"An admirable and unique weapon," said he, "noiseless and of tremendous power. I knew Von Herder, the blind German mechanic, who constructed it to the order of the late Professor Moriarty. For years I have been aware of its existence, though I have never before had the opportunity of handling it. I commend it very specially to your attention, Lestrade, and also the bullets which fit it."

"You can trust us to look after that, Mr. Holmes," said Lestrade, as the whole party moved towards the door. "Anything further to say?"

"Only to ask what charge you intend to prefer?"

"What charge, sir? Why, of course, the attempted murder of Mr. Sherlock Holmes."

"Not so, Lestrade. I do not propose to appear in the matter at all. To you, and to you only, belongs the credit of the remarkable arrest which you have effected. Yes, Lestrade, I congratulate you! With your usual happy mixture of cunning and audacity you have got him."

"Got him! Got whom, Mr. Holmes?"

"The man that the whole force has been seeking in vain— Colonel Sebastian Moran, who shot the Honourable Ronald Adair with an expanding bullet from an air-gun through the open window of the second-floor front of No. 427, Park Lane, upon the 30th of last month. That's the charge, Lestrade. And now, Watson, if you can endure the draught from a broken window, I think that half an hour in my study over a cigar may afford you some profitable amusement."

Our old chambers had been left unchanged through the supervision of Mycroft Holmes and the immediate care of Mrs. Hudson. As I entered I saw, it is true, an unwonted tidiness, but the old landmarks were all in their place. There were the chemical corner and the acid-stained, deal-topped table. There upon a shelf was the row of formidable scrap-books and books of reference which many of our fellow-citizens would have been so glad to burn. The diagrams, the violin-case, and the pipe-rack—even the Persian slipper which contained the tobacco—all met my eyes as I glanced round me. There were two occupants of the room— one Mrs. Hudson, who beamed upon us both as we entered; the other the strange dummy which had played so important a part in the evening's adventures. It was a wax-coloured model of my friend, so admirably done that it was a perfect facsimile. It stood on a small pedestal table with an old dressing-gown of Holmes's so draped round it that the illusion from the street was absolutely perfect.

"I hope you preserved all precautions, Mrs. Hudson?" said Holmes.

"I went to it on my knees, sir, just as you told me."

"Excellent. You carried the thing out very well. Did you observe where the bullet went?"

"Yes, sir. I'm afraid it has spoilt your beautiful bust, for it passed right through the head and flattened itself on the wall. I picked it up from the carpet. Here it is!"

Holmes held it out to me. "A soft revolver bullet, as you perceive, Watson. There's genius in that, for who would expect to find such a thing fired from an air-gun. All right, Mrs. Hudson, I am much obliged for your assistance. And now, Watson, let me see you in your old seat once more, for there are several points which I should like to discuss with you."

He had thrown off the seedy frock-coat, and now he was the Holmes of old in the mouse-coloured dressing-gown which he took from his effigy.

"The old shikari's nerves have not lost their steadiness nor his eyes their keenness," said he, with a laugh, as he inspected the shattered forehead of his bust.

"Plumb in the middle of the back of the head and smack through the brain. He was the best shot in India, and I expect that there are few better in London. Have you heard the name?"

"No, I have not."

"Well, well, such is fame! But, then, if I remember aright, you had not heard the name of Professor James Moriarty, who had one of the great brains of the century. Just give me down my index of biographies from the shelf."

He turned over the pages lazily, leaning back in his chair and blowing great clouds from his cigar.

"My collection of M's is a fine one," said he. "Moriarty himself is enough to make any letter illustrious, and here is Morgan the poisoner, and Merridew of abominable memory, and Mathews, who knocked out my left canine in the waiting-room at Charing Cross, and, finally, here is our friend of to-night."

He handed over the book, and I read: "MORAN, SEBASTIAN, COLONEL. Unemployed. Formerly 1st Bengalore Pioneers. Born London, 1840. Son of Sir Augustus Moran, C.B., once British Minister to Persia. Educated Eton and Oxford. Served in Jowaki Campaign, Afghan Campaign, Charasiab (dispatches), Sherpur, and Cabul. Author of 'Heavy Game of the Western Himalayas,' 1881; 'Three Months in the Jungle,' 1884. Address: Conduit Street. Clubs: The Anglo-Indian, the Tankerville, the Bagatelle Card Club."

On the margin was written, in Holmes's precise hand: "The second most dangerous man in London."

"This is astonishing," said I, as I handed back the volume. "The man's career is that of an honourable soldier."

"It is true," Holmes answered. "Up to a certain point he did well. He was always a man of iron nerve, and the story is still told in India how he crawled down a drain after a wounded man-eating tiger. There are some trees, Watson, which grow to a certain height and then suddenly develop some unsightly eccentricity. You will see it often in humans. I have a theory that the individual represents in his development the whole procession of his ancestors, and that such a sudden turn to good or evil stands for some strong influence which came into the line of his pedigree. The person becomes, as it were, the epitome of the history of his own family."

"It is surely rather fanciful."

"Well, I don't insist upon it. Whatever the cause, Colonel Moran began to go wrong. Without any open scandal he still made India too hot to hold him. He retired, came to London, and again acquired an evil name. It was at this time that he was sought out by Professor Moriarty, to whom for a time he was chief of the staff. Moriarty supplied him liberally with money and used him only in one or two very high-class jobs which no ordinary criminal could have undertaken. You may have some recollection of the death of Mrs. Stewart, of Lauder, in 1887. Not? Well, I am sure Moran was at the bottom of it; but nothing could be proved. So cleverly was the Colonel concealed that even when the Moriarty gang was broken up we could not incriminate him. You remember at that date, when I called upon you in your rooms, how I put up the shutters for fear of air-guns? No doubt you thought me fanciful. I knew exactly what I was doing, for I knew of the existence of this remarkable gun, and I knew also that one of the best shots in the world would be behind it. When we were in Switzerland he followed us with Moriarty, and it was undoubtedly he who gave me that evil five minutes on the Reichenbach ledge.

"You may think that I read the papers with some attention during my sojourn in France, on the look-out for any chance of laying him by the heels. So long as he was free in London my life would really not have been worth living. Night and day the shadow would have been over me, and sooner or later his chance must have come. What could I do? I could not shoot him at sight, or I should myself be in the dock. There was no use appealing to a magistrate. They cannot interfere on the strength of what would appear to them to be a wild suspicion. So I could do nothing. But I watched the criminal news, knowing that sooner or later I should get him. Then came the death of this Ronald Adair. My chance had come at last! Knowing what I did, was it not certain that Colonel Moran had done it? He had played cards with the lad; he had followed him home from the club; he had shot him through the open window. There was not a doubt of it. The bullets alone are enough to put his head in a noose. I came over at once. I was seen by the sentinel, who would, I knew, direct the Colonel's attention to my presence. He could not fail to connect my sudden return with his crime and to be terribly alarmed. I was sure that he would make an attempt to get me out of the way AT ONCE, and would bring round his murderous weapon for that purpose. I left him an excellent mark in the window, and, having warned the police that they might be needed—by the way, Watson, you spotted their presence in that doorway with unerring accuracy—I took up what seemed to me to be a judicious post for observation, never dreaming that he would choose the same spot for his attack. Now, my dear Watson, does anything remain for me to explain?"

"Yes," said I. "You have not made it clear what was Colonel Moran's motive in murdering the Honourable Ronald Adair."

"Ah! my dear Watson, there we come into those realms of conjecture where the most logical mind may be at fault. Each may form his own hypothesis upon the present evidence, and yours is as likely to be correct as mine."

"You have formed one, then?"

"I think that it is not difficult to explain the facts. It came out in evidence that Colonel Moran and young Adair had between them won a considerable amount of money. Now, Moran undoubtedly played foul—of that I have long been aware. I believe that on the day of the murder Adair had discovered that Moran was cheating. Very likely he had spoken to him privately, and had threatened to expose him unless he voluntarily resigned his membership of the club and promised not to play cards again. It is unlikely that a youngster like Adair would at once make a hideous scandal by exposing a well-known man so much older than himself. Probably he acted as I suggest. The exclusion from his clubs would mean ruin to Moran, who lived by his ill-gotten card gains. He therefore murdered Adair, who at the time was endeavouring to work out how much money he should himself return, since he could not profit by his partner's foul play. He locked the door lest the ladies should surprise him and insist upon knowing what he was doing with these names and coins. Will it pass?"

"I have no doubt that you have hit upon the truth."

"It will be verified or disproved at the trial. Meanwhile, come what may, Colonel Moran will trouble us no more, the famous air-gun of Von Herder will embellish the Scotland Yard Museum, and once again Mr. Sherlock Holmes is free to devote his life to examining those interesting little problems which the complex life of London so plentifully presents."

Made in the USA
San Bernardino, CA
13 March 2020